Unfinished Business

Banham cocked his gun. The remaining two men came up off the floor side by side, guns smoking. Banham fired. The nearest man toppled over as the slug thudded into his chest and broke two ribs before piercing his heart. The last man was already levelling his gun. Banham shaded him, fired first, and a torrent of blood erupted from his adversary's mouth when the half-inch chunk of lead tore out his throat. . . .

Unfinished Business

Corba Sunman

A Black Horse Western

ROBERT HALE

© Corba Sunman 2019
First published in Great Britain 2019

ISBN 978-0-7198-2973-4

The Crowood Press
The Stable Block
Crowood Lane
Ramsbury
Marlborough
Wiltshire SN8 2HR

www.bhwesterns.com

Robert Hale is an imprint
of The Crowood Press

Typeset by
Derek Doyle & Associates, Shaw Heath
Printed and bound in Great Britain by
4Bind Ltd, Stevenage, SG1 2XT

ONE

The sound of a bullet crackled in Dale Banham's left ear as he bent low in his saddle to unfasten the gate leading into the yard of the HB cow spread in west Texas. He promptly forgot about the gate and threw himself out of the saddle, hitting the ground with his left shoulder and rolling aside before regaining his feet with his pistol coming to hand. He looked towards the ranch house and saw a puff of gun smoke drifting from an open downstairs window, and a pale face peering at him from inside the house. He slid his pistol back into its holster and lifted his hand in a gesture of friendliness, but ducked when a gun flashed at the window.

He vaulted the gate and ran towards the house, shooting at the window as he charged across the yard. His boots thudded on the small porch and he peered in through the window, his gun muzzle angling to cover the interior of the room. A figure was crouched in a corner, and he realized with a start of surprise that it was a woman. He had been expecting to see his sister Hannah, but this woman was a stranger, and she was holding a pistol in her right hand and looked as if she knew how to handle it.

Banham covered her with his .45 Colt Peacemaker.

'Put down the gun, Ma'am,' he told her gently. 'I'm friendly.'

'I doubt if there is a friendly male in the whole of Benton County,' she responded in a harsh tone. 'Who are you, mister?' Her keen blue eyes took in his tall figure, travel-stained range garb, and rested for a moment on his pistol. She nodded as she centred her gaze on his rugged face. 'I won't lose my bet if I say you must be Dale Banham, my friend Hannah's brother.'

'That's a good bet. I'm only thankful that your shooting isn't as good as your gambling.'

'Shucks, I wasn't aiming to hit you. Hannah told me a week ago that she was expecting you to show up.'

'How in tarnation did she figure that out? And where is she?'

'She went out the back door just before I spotted you out front. She saw someone sneaking around the barn and went to deter him.'

'So there is trouble around here, huh?

'That's why you're here, ain't it?' She was good-looking, under thirty years old, and had a smile on her generous mouth. But her pale eyes held shadows of worry and a splash of fear. 'I'm Aggie Browning. Hadn't you better go out back and see where Hannah is? There's been trouble around here for weeks, and it's getting worse.'

Banham entered the house and went through the kitchen to the back door. He peered through the window beside the door and studied the back yard. Two barns were to the rear, and he saw his sister Hannah standing in the half-open doorway of the right-hand barn, talking to a tall, lean man dressed like a cattleman.

He opened the door and stepped outside, calling his sister by name. She turned to look at him and then came running across the yard to push herself into his arms.

'Dale, you're here at last.' Tears of relief ran down her cheeks, and he held her at arm's length to look at her.

'What happened to your husband?' he asked. 'Bill Rix, if I remember correctly. I'm sorry I missed your wedding. At that time I was occupied with a situation I couldn't leave.'

'That's the same old story, Dale.' Her blue eyes blinked rapidly and her expression changed, 'Bill was killed six months ago. We had callers that night – six of them – and he couldn't fight them off. Didn't you get my letter?'

'If I had I would have come running.' He glanced over her shoulder at the man standing motionless beside the barn. 'Who's your friend?'

'He's Larry Hogan – owns a cattle spread to the north. He's been a good neighbour to me since Bill died.'

'Well I'm here now, and you won't need anyone else while I'm around.'

'Are you still a lawman?' she looked into his eyes, and a sigh escaped her as he nodded.

'What else? I'm a deputy US Marshal now, and I'm here because reports of bad trouble around Benton County have been filtering through to headquarters. But keep that under your hat, Hannah, because I want to make an investigation under cover, if that's possible.'

'I'll just see Larry off. Have you met Aggie?'

'That fire cracker you call a friend?' He nodded. 'She nigh shot me through the head as I opened your gate.'

'If she fired at you and missed then she wasn't aiming to kill you.' Hannah turned and hurried back to the barn.

Banham returned to the kitchen and found Aggie standing just inside the door, now holding a Winchester .44-40 in her capable hands. She turned and walked through to the big front living room before swinging to face him. He paused as she put her left shoulder to the front wall beside the porch door and watched the yard as they talked.

'I'm glad you're here, for Hannah's sake,' she said. 'She's in a highly nervous state right now, and needs someone to lean on, but from what she's told me about you, I am wondering why you didn't show up when she wrote you about her troubles.'

'I didn't hear from her.' He shook his head. 'But I'm here now to run my eye over the situation.' He paused. She did not speak but watched him keenly, her expressive eyes filled with accusation. 'We have a lot of crime in other parts of Texas,' he continued, 'and there's a vast area to cover. We never have enough men to cope with duty, which means that those of us fighting crime are overrun with work. Where did you learn to shoot?'

She smiled, showing perfectly even, white teeth. 'My father runs the general store in town, and as he didn't have a son – just me – it was my daily chore to shoot the rats trying to eat us out of house and home. Pa gets to hear just about everything that happens in the county. He's not happy with what he's learned, and he has been talking about pulling stakes and moving on. He's certain that a big operator has moved in somewhere on the range, like the rats that besiege us, and is now calling all the shots.'

'Was Bill's killer caught?'

'Not that we know of, but then Pa doesn't go a lot on Sheriff Bain, and I've never known my old man to be wrong about anyone when he makes a judgement of character.'

'That's interesting. We must talk some more, Aggie, but right now take a look across the yard and tell me if you recognize the two men fixing to visit.'

She gazed across the dust pan of the yard to the gate. Watching her expressive face, Banham saw bleakness filter into her eyes and she lifted her rifle into the aim. He pushed down the weapon.

'There's no need to start shooting,' he reproved. 'Just tell me if you recognize them.'

'It's that dratted Sheriff Bain and his nasty deputy Lopez. Why are they sniffing around here? Lopez thinks he's the world's greatest lover just because he can play a guitar and sing well. He was outside the yard one night around midnight last week, singing and playing, until I put a slug through his guitar. We haven't seen him around since, and I was beginning to hope I'd clipped him and laid him up. But by the look of him I guess he got lucky, but now he's back again, bold as brass and full of sass.'

'Do you greet all your callers with a slug?' he asked, and she smiled.

'A gal needs to cull the herd at times or she'd be knee deep in singing cowboys, and we'd never get any work done. But be careful of Chain Bain, Dale. He's deep as the ocean, and a man like that, Pa says, is one to watch out for.'

'Chain Bain,' Banham repeated. 'Is that given name for real?'

Aggie grinned and shook her head. 'It's a part of his reputation. They call him Chain because he's faster than chain-lightning.'

'Is that a fact,' he smiled. 'Then I'd better start praying that he's a good lawman, huh?' He moved to the door. 'I'll meet him outside and introduce myself to him. I'm chain-lightning myself when it comes to assessing a stranger. What happened to old Sheriff Tate?

'He died on the trail to Dolan's cattle spread, the Big D. That would be three years ago. Bain showed up about that time, and nobody else wanted the job of sheriff so he got the most votes. Thinking about it, I have a sneaking feeling the election was rigged, and life has gone downhill since Bain took over.'

Banham hitched his gun-belt and stepped out to the porch. He glanced at the window beside the door and saw Aggie's face there, her rifle visible. He made a quick motion with his right hand and she moved back in the room and was lost to sight from outside, but he knew she would still be covering the yard and realized that he would need to have a heart-to-heart talk with her or she would soon be acting as a volunteer deputy to him. He cringed at the thought and moved to the edge of the porch, watching the two newcomers coming across the yard.

It was easy to identify the sheriff because Lopez was from south of the border and wore Mexican clothes, right down to the cruel Spanish rowels on his spurs. His broad-brimmed sombrero shaded his dark face but Banham could see that he was a handsome man. There was an arrogant swing to his shoulders, but his top lip held a cruel twist. His right hand was close to the butt of the pistol on his hip and his quick eyes watched his surroundings as if he expected some desperado to spring out of cover at him. He wore dark blue denims and a charro jacket.

The sheriff, law badge glinting on his blue shirt, was powerfully built, with massive shoulders that looked all muscle, and bronzed arms that gave an impression he could kill a wild steer with his bare

11

hands. He was wearing Texas leg chaps and an almost shapeless black Stetson that was set low over his dark eyes. His blue shirt had faded to white in places and he had a pair of pistols, one on each hip; that looked like earlier models of a Colt. Neither Bain nor Lopez was older than thirty.

They reined up at the edge of the porch, and did not speak while they looked Banham over. He remained silent until it became clear that they wanted him to speak first and he smiled.

'Morning, gents,' he greeted. 'You're the county law, huh? From what I heard about the goings on around here I reckoned there was no law department hereabouts at all.'

'You got more sass than a kid, and I reckon you're long past that age in your life,' Bain replied. 'Either you've got a naturally loose lip or you're hacking for trouble.'

'And we're the men to dish that out,' said Lopez in a silky tone. He spoke American with no trace of an accent. 'Are you looking for trouble, *amigo?*'

'Not here, on my own doorstep.' Banham grinned. 'But you were certainly inviting it when you were out there beyond the gate past midnight, playing your guitar and singing. I reckon you must have been breaking some law or other, and I would have done something about you if I had been here then.'

Bain burst into a guffaw of laughter. 'I knew your Mex antics would get you in trouble one day, Lopez.' He pounded his right fist on his saddle-horn.

'Damned if I won't look up the laws of this county to see if there is anything that will stop you howling like a tomcat on a roof while you're twanging that banjo of yours.' His merriment vanished like leaves in an autumn gale and his face was set in its usual form when he turned his eyes back to Banham. 'Who are you, mister, and what's your business here?' His tone was hoarse and filled with menace, eyes glittering like a predator moving in for the kill. 'As far as I'm concerned you're a stranger, and I don't like that breed at all.'

'My sister Hannah owns this spread, and I'm here to spend some time with her. It's my first visit in five years, and I'm hopeful of getting some rest and good home cooking.'

'Where did you come from, and what do you do for a living?' Lopez flung at him sharply.

'I don't consider my past being any of your business. I'm not penniless, and I can pay my way while I'm here.'

'Not if I take a dislike to you.' Bain grinned. 'You better watch your step around here, mister, or you'll be getting the rest you reckon you need in a box under six feet of rangeland.'

Annie came out to the porch and paused at Banham's left shoulder.

'What's your business here, Sheriff?' she demanded. 'You're not welcome, and that goes for your deputy. Stay away from us unless it's your duty to call.'

'I'm here on duty,' Bain said with a sneering grin

that sent instant heat through Banham's stomach. 'I got a complaint from Matt Dolan that his fence over by Coyote Creek, between your range and his, has been cut, and some of his stock are on your grass.'

'Not again!' Annie shook her head in disgust. 'He should tend his fences better. Why would I want to cut his wire?'

'It's not my job to go into the why or wherefore of any complaint that comes into my office.' Bain shifted impatiently in his saddle. 'I'm here to warn you about making trouble with your big neighbour. That trail can only lead to disaster. Pull in your horns before you go too far. It would be hopeless for you to try and use the fact that you're a woman as a lever against the local cattlemen. You'll get trampled underfoot if Dolan climbs into his big saddle and comes rampaging after you.'

'It's easy to see whose side you're on,' said Annie fiercely. 'Now listen to my complaint. Dolan is cutting his own fences to let his cows cross my range to the river. He's short of water because he's running too much beef on his range. Take a ride down to my west line and look for yourself. Any of Dolan's steers on my grass will be living high on the hog, eating my feed and drinking my water. Let me see you do something about that, Sheriff.'

Bain opened his mouth to remonstrate but Banham cut him off.

'While I'm here, Sheriff, I'll be responsible for this spread, so in future you can address your remarks to me, and if you take Annie's complaint to

Dolan be sure to tell him that if I see any of his stock on our range after this he'll be sued in court for the cost of the water and feed he's stealing from us.'

'I can't go to a man like Dolan with a message like that!' Bain leaned forward in his saddle, scowling.

'But I can, and I will,' Banham said. 'Now why don't you get out of here with your Mexican song bird and stop wasting our time?'

'You go too far,' rasped Lopez, his bronzed face twisting into harsh lines. He dropped his right hand to his gun butt and it slid out of its holster with practised ease.

Banham saw the deputy's action and leaned slightly to the left as he palmed his pistol and covered the Mexican. Lopez was still lifting his gun into the aim when he realized that Banham had completed his draw, and he heard the three clicks that signified Banham was ready to start shooting. Banham's face was calm, his eyes glittering as Lopez faltered.

'You'd better drop the gun or tomorrow you'll be attending your funeral,' Banham said.

'Stop this,' Bain said sharply. 'Throw down your gun, Lopez. Can't you see what you're up against?'

When Lopez ignored the warning, Bain reached out swiftly and chopped the edge of his left hand against the Mexican's gun wrist. The pistol fell to the ground. Banham eased forward the hammer of his gun, but Lopez was enraged, and his natural caution had deserted him. He turned on Bain.

'Stay out of this. It's personal.'

Bain stared into his deputy's contorted face and shrugged. He jerked his horse away from Lopez's side.

'It's your funeral,' he said.

Lopez reached into his waistband and produced a two-shot derringer. Banham set his gun hand into motion, drew his pistol again and fired in the same instant. Lopez dropped his gun as if it had suddenly become too hot to hold, and gripped his blood-dripping fingers. He stared at Banham in disbelief. In the three years he had been a deputy he had not found one gunslinger fast enough to match him. But Banham had beaten him with no effort. The knowledge sank into Lopez's mind and took root like a festering sore.

Bain gigged his horse forward and herded Lopez towards the gate, and Banham, gun in hand, stood watching until sheriff and deputy had departed.

'That sure was some shooting!' Aggie declared, appearing at Hannah's side. 'I haven't seen the like since Wild Bill Hickok came to town a couple of years back. He was law dealing then, and killed four bank robbers from an even break. They went down like flies right outside our store. We could sure do with some one of Hickok's calibre now to take on this set-up.'

Banham watched the two lawmen ride out of sight before holstering his gun. He looked at his sister, who was watching him intently, and shook his head.

'What am I going to do about you?' he

demanded. 'I've got to go to town now, and I don't like the idea of leaving you out here alone.'

'Don't forget about me,' Aggie said stoutly, and Banham smiled.

'I don't think I'll ever forget you,' he replied. 'You'd better go back to the store and stay there. It ain't good policy to get mixed up in somebody else's fight.'

'But I can't leave Hannah here alone,' Aggie protested.

'She won't be here alone. I'll take her into town with me, and she'll stay there until this trouble is over.'

'I can't leave here,' Hannah protested. 'I've got stock to look after.'

'Just do as I say. I'll find someone in town to come out here for a week or two to take care of the place.'

Hannah shrugged, aware that her brother would not retreat from the stand he was taking. 'I'll get some things together to take with me,' she said submissively. 'Al Carson does odd jobs around town, and he'll come out here like you want. He lives in a shack on the outskirts of town – on the left as you ride in from this side.'

'We'll look in on him when we get there,' Aggie said. 'You'll come and stay with me at the store while you're in town, won't you, Hannah?'

'Only if you promise not to shoot rats from your bed,' Hannah countered, and they laughed.

Banham saddled two horses to a two-wheeled rig in the barn and took it around to the front door of the ranch house. He gave his horse a pan of crushed oats and a half bucket of water from the well. The girls emerged from the house and got into the rig. Banham swung into his saddle. Hannah cracked her whip and they set out for Clear Water Creek.

Two miles out from the little cow town, a rifle, firing from cover, put a slug through the crown of Banham's hat. . . .

TWO

When Banham's Stetson was flipped from his head by a slug, he dived from his saddle and buried his nose in the dirt, but got to his feet instantly, snatched his rifle from its saddle boot, and ran to the rig, where both girls were sitting in a frozen attitude of shock.

'Stay put,' he rasped.

Aggie sat up and reached for her rifle, eyes searching her surroundings for the ambusher. She saw furtive movement on the nearest skyline and lifted her rifle into the aim.

'Watch my shot,' she called to Banham. 'I've got him spotted.'

She fired, and Banham saw her slug ricochet from a rock a hundred yards away. A figure sprang up and changed position, and Banham snapped a quick shot. The bullet caught the figure, broke his stride, and spun him around before he dropped out of sight. Banham ran forward, jacking another shell into his long gun. He reached the crest where the

19

man had fallen, heard the sound of rapidly receding hoofs, and saw a rider moving away fast, hunched in his saddle.

Banham lifted his rifle to his shoulder, fired, and the man pitched out of leather. He watched the figure for several moments, noted that he did not stir, and then ran towards him. The man was on his face, arms out-flung. He had a bullet hole between his shoulder blades. He was range clad – denim trousers, Stetson, leather vest, and a red neckerchief tied at his throat. He was dead, his eyes beginning to glaze. Banham turned his attention to the horse, which had halted a couple of yards ahead and was grazing. The animal was branded with a big D.

He was searching the man's pockets when the rig drew up close by, his horse tied to the back. Hannah jumped out and came forward to view the kill.

'It's Tod Nesbit. He rides for Dolan, who owns the Big D,' said Aggie promptly.

'He was on this range five years ago,' Banham said quietly. 'His name was Fargo then – Mick Fargo. He rode with the Holt Miller outlaw gang, but he was riding for Big D.'

'Dolan is a brute,' Aggie said, 'and he acts like one. He comes into the store quite often, and I can't bear his eyes on me. My pa doesn't like him, but he can't afford to turn away trade. The Big D is the biggest cattle spread in the county and has nigh twenty men on the payroll.'

'I'll take Fargo back to where he came from,'

Banham decided. 'How do I get to Dolan's spread?'

'Ride back to our place and follow the trail north,' Hannah said. 'It'll take you right into Dolan's place. But you're not thinking of going there alone, are you, Dale?'

'Don't worry about me,' he replied, his eyes turning bleak. 'It's only common courtesy to take a man you've killed back to his employer.'

'Did Fargo know you on your previous visit to this neck of the woods?' Aggie asked.

Banham nodded. 'I arrested him once and jailed him in town, but someone busted him out. It sure looks like his luck ran out this time.'

'Be careful,' Hannah said, and she was chilled by the fact that his glance was like that of a stranger. She fell silent, shaking her head.

'Take it easy around town,' he warned. 'Don't take any chances. Something bad is going on. It's got to do with me when I was here before, considering what's happened. I'll see you when I get back, and I'll be as quick as I can.'

Both girls nodded silently, each too anxious to speak. It was not until he had tied the cadaver to its saddle, mounted his horse and turned away with a slight lift of a hand, leading the dead man's horse, that Hannah found her tongue and uttered a simple prayer for his safety.

'Now I know how you must have felt about your brother all those years ago,' Aggie said. 'I'll follow him if you like, with my rifle. If he gets into a tight spot I'll pitch in.'

21

'Don't even think things like that. He'd probably hear you on his back trail, and you might wind up dead.' Hannah shuddered. 'Let's get on to town. Dale makes his own luck, and we've got to abide with that.'

'You drive and I'll keep my rifle handy,' Aggie replied.

Hannah cracked the whip and they went on to town, but both girls were thinking of the lone man on his dangerous trail, going forward to do his job against overwhelming odds. . . .

Banham was thoughtful as he rode north. He had his teeth set in the trouble and would not let go no matter where the trail led. He cast his mind back to his last visit to this area, and several names came to mind. He made a mental note of them, and came to the conclusion that, given his normal luck, he could soon deal with this spot of bother.

Three hours later he topped a rise and looked down on the headquarters of a big cattle ranch. The sun was reaching for the western horizon, its slanting rays highlighting every foot of the range. Set on a knoll was a ranch house, made of adobe bricks, four-square and prominent, overlooking barns and smaller buildings – three corrals, two bunk houses and a cook shack; the latter buildings all connected by a sun-hardened path that was roofed along its length.

Men were converging on the shack from all over the ranch. A curl of smoke was spilling out of its smoke stack, smudging the roseate sky as the wind toyed with it. A woman was dismounting from a white horse in front of the house, and she paused to exchange words with an old man seated on a rocking chair on the porch. A wrangler was in the nearest corral with his last horse of the day, breaking it in, and little puffs of dust rose at the incessant pounding of hoofs while the wrangler's cries echoed and re-echoed across the range.

Banham's eyes glistened as he looked at the familiar scene. The cowpokes who had already collected their meal were settling down on the grass in front of the cook shack to eat, and the cook, with a helper, was attending to the needs of the rest of the crew as they turned up.

Banham's horse picked its way towards the knoll, followed by the animal carrying the body. He moved at a walk, and some of the feeding crew eyed him speculatively as he proceeded. When it was obvious that he was heading for the house, a squat, burly cowpoke put aside his plate and arose to confront Banham – dusty and sweating, blocky; looking as if nothing human on earth could stretch him out.

'Say, where do you think you're going?' the cowpoke demanded.

'This is the Big D cattle ranch, ain't it?' Banham replied.

'It sure is, but strangers ain't permitted to come and go as they please. I'm Jake Dillman, the foreman, and I want to know who you are and what your business is with Mr Dolan before you move another step. And who's the dead man across the saddle of your lead horse?'

'I've got business with Dolan.'

'So tell me about it.' Dillman set himself, his right hand dropping to his gun butt.

'I'll tell Dolan, and he'll tell you about it if he has a mind to.' Banham kept moving, and Dillman suddenly found himself in danger of being run down by Banham's horse. He jumped aside, his manner changing, and reached for his holstered pistol.

Banham twisted in his saddle, saw Dillman's elbow bend as he drew his gun, and pulled his own weapon. It was in his hand, ready-cocked, before Dillman could complete his move. Dillman froze. Banham grinned.

'That was a bad mistake on your part,' Banham observed. 'Now you can push your gun back into your holster and go back to your chuck, or you can continue your draw, but if you do you won't need another mouthful of grub – ever.'

'I reckon you can go on to the house this once,' said Dillman grudgingly, and he thrust his gun deep into the holster.

Banham continued, watching Dillman across his left shoulder. The foreman remained motionless, staring after Banham until the two horses reached the porch in front of the ranch house. When Banham dismounted and stepped on to the porch, Dillman went back to his meal.

A man stepped out of the house and stood on the porch, watching Banham tethering his horse. He was small but wide-shouldered, dressed in a blue store suit; grey Stetson, and well-polished riding boots. He was past middle age, and his mahogany-coloured face was weathered, his narrowed blue eyes etched by many small wrinkles. If he was carrying a gun then it was hidden on his person.

'Howdy?' he greeted. 'I happened to be watching from the window and saw Dillman brace you. He sure pulled his horns in when you made your draw, and he didn't move a muscle while you came on up here. Who's the dead man?'

'I was told his name was Nesbit and that he's one of your riders. But I knew him around here about five years ago as Fargo. He used to ride with Holt Miller's outlaw gang, but made the mistake of hanging around too long, and he was on hand to ambush me earlier today.'

'Whereabouts did he make his try?' Dolan's seamed face had hardened, and his eyes became mere points of brilliance.

'First off, I'm Dale Banham, deputy US Marshal. My sister Hannah runs the Double H cattle spread. Her husband, Bill Rix, was killed some months ago and his killer has not been caught. I came back to this range today after an absence of some five years, and I sure put my hand into a hornets' nest. I figure that Fargo recognized me and decided to put me out of my saddle.'

'That's the way it's going around here these days.' Dolan's expression remained unchanged. 'Dog eats dog. But Nesbit was supposed to be riding the north line.' His face relaxed and he nodded. 'I'll have a

25

word with Dillman later.'

'Get Dillman over here right now and we'll both talk to him.' A rough edge sounded in Banham's tone.

'You sure talk like a lawman.' Dolan nodded. He reached into a back pocket of his pants, produced a small-calibre pistol, and grinned when Banham made a fast draw and covered him with the muzzle of his .45.

'That's some draw,' Dolan said. 'I'd say you're in the class of Doc Holliday. He was real slick when he wasn't coughing up his lungs. And you could stand up with Wyatt Earp. I guess the bad men around here better watch their step, huh? And you'll have to watch your back when the word on you gets out.'

'It's already got out,' Banham said easily. 'What's the trouble between you and my sister Hannah? I made the down payment for her when she took on the ranch, so I've got a personal interest in it.'

'There's no trouble between your sister and me. Sheriff Bain was out here last evening and I mentioned that my fence had been cut and some of my cows had drifted on to your grass. I ain't got around to talking to Hannah yet.'

'And Bain went to my sister and said you told him she was responsible, huh? So what kind of a game is Bain playing? I'll have a chat with him when I get to town.'

Banham fell silent when a woman appeared in the doorway behind Dolan. She was much older that he had thought when he saw her dismounting from the white horse when he rode in earlier. Tall and slender, she had an attractive face and alert brown eyes, and gazed at him with undisguised interest. He felt a start of surprise when he suddenly recognized her as Lola Brent – five years ago he had been more than half in love with her.

'Sorry to interrupt,' she said, 'but it's time Uncle Ben came in for his meal.'

Banham glanced at the motionless figure seated in the rocking chair beside the door. It was an old man, and he seemed to be unaware of his surroundings. Dolan glanced at the woman.

'This is my wife Lola,' he said. 'Shake hands with US Marshal Banham, Lola. He's in the county to put down the trouble we're getting.'

Lola Dolan extended her hand and Banham grasped her fingers. She permitted the merest touch, smiling at him, but her eyes were devoid of expression, and Banham felt a pang strike through him when he realized that she did not want him to recognize her here and now. She turned to the old man in the chair, reached out to grasp his thin shoulders and pulled him gently to his feet. He went without protest and she led him into the house. He walked with a shambling gait, and seemed to have problems with his balance.

'That's Deke, my brother,' Dolan said. 'He's been like that since he fell off his horse, and I don't think he'll ever recover.'

'Bad luck,' Banham commented. Broken-down cowboys were a familiar sight in the townships of the West, victims of a tough, hazardous calling.

Dolan walked out to the porch and fired his gun into the air, sending a series of echoes across the valley. Dillman looked towards the house and Dolan waved to him. The tough foreman came immediately. Dolan slid his gun into his pocket, and smiled when he met Banham's gaze.

Dillman paused beside the body on the horse, grasped a handful of the dead man's hair, and lifted the head to peer at the stiff features. He twisted his own head and glanced at the porch, where Dolan and Banham stood watching him.

'It's Nesbit,' he said in an unemotional tone, his eyes boring into Banham's gaze. 'Did you kill him?'

'He ambushed me.' Banham explained where the incident had taken place.

'I sent him this morning to ride the north line.' Dillman came on to the porch. 'Why would he ambush you?'

'We met about five years ago. He was a member of an outlaw gang and I got the drop on him. I'm wondering how he knew I was back in this county.'

'And how did he get a job on my payroll?' Dolan rapped.

'I'll find out,' Banham said. 'I'm on my way to town now, and I'll set the wheels turning.'

Dolan walked into the house, followed by Dillman. Banham could hear Dolan's voice as he gave orders to his foreman about business on the ranch.

Lola's voice cut into their conversation. 'I'm

riding into town now,' she said in a tone that discouraged argument.

'Don't leave until Banham has got clear,' Dolan rasped.

Lola appeared in the doorway, and compressed her lips when she saw Banham still standing within earshot. She stepped on to the porch and closed the door.

'You should be pleased I'll be riding to town with you.' She brushed by Banham and hurried off the porch, turning her face towards him as she reached the front corner of the house. 'I'll get my horse. Stay close to this end of the porch and join me when I ride to the gate. I'll keep between you and the house as much as I can until you're clear of the spread.'

He nodded and went to his horse, led it along the front of the porch, and stood waiting for Lola to return. It seemed an age before she appeared, and her face was grim as she motioned for him to join her. He swung into his saddle and kneed the horse forward to her side as she rode across the yard, glancing over his shoulder at the house when he heard Dolan's voice.

'Where in hell do you think you're going, Lola?'

'I told you I needed to ride into town.' She spoke without turning her face towards her husband, and there was a sharp note in her voice.

'Are you planning to ride with Banham?'

'It sure looks that way.'

'There could be shooting at him, and his

29

enemies won't care if you're with him. He's a marked man, and he knows it.'

'You've got enough men on the spread to make sure I get to town without danger.' Lola rapped. 'You're always talking up trouble these days, and it's getting tiresome. But I think Banham is man enough to get me through in one piece.'

'OK, cut along now, and you make sure she suffers no harm, Banham.'

They continued across the yard, and Banham saw the rest of the crew, some still eating their meal, taking an interest in what was going on in the yard. A couple of them fingered their holstered guns, and Banham tensed and prepared for action, although the time and the place were not to his liking. But they reached the gate without incident. Banham glanced back at the house and saw Dolan watching moodily from the porch. Dillman was on his way back to his interrupted meal.

'No one will try anything against you while we're together,' Lola said. 'Let's push on, and you can relax until I leave you in town.'

'Why are you going against your husband? He doesn't look like a man who will let his wife overrule him.'

'What have you been doing these past five years?' She changed the subject abruptly, and smiled when he glanced at her, her teeth gleaming in the sunlight. He could see why he had almost fallen in love with her in the old days, and closed his mind to memories that came thrusting to the surface. That part of his life was dead, and he would not resurrect it. Life was still too painful to be given any chance of overwhelming his thoughts with memories.

'Law dealing, that's all. There's never been anything more in my life – just the pure and simple hunting down of bad men. Do me a favour and change the subject, Lola. Tell me what you've done since I last saw you. How did you become involved with a man like Dolan?'

'That's something I don't want to talk about.' Her voice became shrill and cut across his hearing. 'It was a bad mistake and I'm trying to forget it.'

'It's like that, huh?' He shook his head in sympathy.

'I'm so desperate to get away from my present life I'd pay a killer to shoot Dolan.'

'Hey, you're talking to the wrong man about that subject.'

'I'm not going to ask you to do it. If I wait long enough you'll probably have to kill him anyway.'

'I'll play that particular hand when the time comes,' he said philosophically.

'And I can't wait for it to arrive.' She glanced over her shoulder at their back trail, and uttered a gasp. 'Hey, take a look behind. We're being followed. Dolan is a real sidewinder. He's sent three of his men to get you, and he's used me to set you up.'

Banham glanced along their back trail and saw three riders following. They were not attempting to catch up, and Banham's face took on a bleak expression.

'You'd better push on for town and I'll take care of this problem when you're clear.'

'No! I'll stay. I can't believe Dolan would come out into the open like this.'

'I want you to do as you're told without argument, so pull out and keep riding until you hit town. I'll follow you shortly. Just tell me where you hang out in town and I'll look you up.'

Lola sighed and shook her head, her teeth nipping her bottom lip in frustration.

'You're wasting time,' she retorted in a low, determined tone. 'Get to work on those range scum. 'You're going to have to fight them, either now or when the showdown comes. Dolan is playing for big stakes, and he won't let anyone stop him. The only way you'll be able to beat him is to get a big posse behind you, and be careful who you pick to back you.' She looked over her shoulder again, and when she spoke there was urgency in her tone. 'They're coming at a run now, and two of them are holding guns. You'll be up to your neck in them in a couple of minutes.'

THREE

At her words, Banham acted instinctively. He leaned sideways towards her and slapped the rump of her horse with such force the animal almost jumped a foot, and the next instant it was running with Lola clinging to the saddle and trying to control it. Banham faced the riders. They were deploying, drifting apart, and gun smoke flared around them as they started shooting. He heard crackling lead zipping around him and returned fire, his teeth clenched, his mind and body ready for action.

Aware that he wanted a prisoner – someone who could give him background information on the local situation – he aimed to wound, not to kill – but the shooting was rapid and accurate, and he took closer aim, tasting gun smoke when he fired. He sighted on the right-hand figure and squeezed off a shot. The man threw up his arms and was swept out of his saddle by the questing lead. The other two riders swung away and made for cover, and Banham sent shots at them as they pulled out of range. One disappeared into rough ground, and the other, following quickly, took a hit in his right shoulder blade, and was drooping over his saddle-horn when he disappeared from sight.

Banham guided his horse with his knees. His eyes were narrowed, his reflexes leaping. He saw the head and shoulders of a man appear in the front of the rough ground where the gunmen had disappeared, and snapped a shot at him. The bullet struck the man's rifle and tore it out of his hands. He dropped out of sight with another bullet tugging at his hat brim.

The sound of shooting came to Banham from the direction in which Lola had gone. He looked ahead and saw gun smoke drifting. Figures were in sight at extreme range. There were three riders closing in on the figure he recognized as Lola. She had apparently fired her pistol to attract his attention. He turned his horse and used his spurs to ride fast towards her.

Slugs snarled around him from his rear, where the survivors of the first attack had sought cover. Banham hunched in his saddle to minimize his target area and urged his horse to greater effort. The animal lengthened its stride, and a moment later he heard the smack of lead striking horseflesh. The horse squealed and tremored, then fell headlong, legs threshing. Banham kicked his feet clear of his stirrups and rolled clear. When he regained his feet the horse was dead.

He looked around and saw a horse grazing, its

rider lying several yards away. He took his saddle-
bags from his mount and pulled his Winchester
from the saddle boot. There was no sign of life on
the range as he set out fast for the grazing horse,
agitated by the way he had been fooled by Dolan's
men. But he was certain that in time, when he had
learned all the facts of this local trouble, he would
swing into action and do his duty. But now he had
to locate Lola and get her safely to town.

As he reached the grazing horse a rifle cracked
and the animal dropped instantly. Banham scrambled into cover and began to search for the position
of the gunman. Evening was drawing in and
shadows were getting long on the ground. He
spotted a puff of gun smoke drifting from a brushy
area, and began to stalk the spot. A figure suddenly
arose from the brush and ran to the right, making
for better cover. Banham lifted his rifle and fired
instantly. The man pitched over on to his left side
and remained motionless.

Banham went forward with his rifle covering the
man. He saw from several yards away that his bullet
had killed, and he went in close to check. He recognized the man as one of those having a meal
recently at Dolan's spread, and looked around for
the dead man's horse; found it in a depression in
the brush. He mounted and set off at a canter for
the spot where he had last seen Lola.

The sun was almost below the western horizon
when he reached a spot where hoofs had beaten
down the grass. He had noted the prints of Lola's

horse before they left the yard of Dolan's ranch, and he found some clear prints left by the animal. There were three sets of unknown prints around, but he ignored them, concentrating on Lola's mount, and was still following them north when darkness fell.

He stood in rapt concentration for several minutes, thinking over the aspects of the situation, and then made camp. He ate hard tack from his meagre supply, drank water before turning in on the dead man's bedroll, and slept dreamlessly until the sun showed itself above the eastern horizon.

Within minutes of rising, Banham was in the saddle, following Lola's horse's hoof prints. In the early morning he had no difficulty locating the faint marks of a horse having passed only hours before, and when he came upon an unblemished outline of a horse shoe in dust in a wild animal scrape, he dismounted to examine it. He recognized it instantly, and looked around at his surroundings in an attempt to determine Lola's direction. There were no other tracks around, and he wondered how she had escaped the attentions of the gunmen he had last seen around her.

He cast around for more prints, and eventually found a continuous trail that was heading southwest in the direction of Clear Water Creek. The new tracks had been made by Lola's horse, and he followed them at a canter, sighting the cattle town around noon. He rode into the collection of buildings fronting Main Street, which he had last seen five years before, and was puzzling over where Lola had been during the night when he spotted her horse hitched to a rail near the bank. He rode in beside it and hitched his mount. The banker's house was next to the bank, and he recalled that Lola had told him she was friendly with the banker's daughter and often stayed with her when in town.

Banham paused for a moment to look around the street. He saw the sheriff approaching him, right hand down by his holstered gun butt and his fierce expression showing that he was looking for trouble.

'I was wondering when you were gonna show up, Marshal,' Bain called. 'Where you been all night? I saw your sister earlier and she told me about you being a State law man. What's the big idea, sneaking into my county and not informing me of your presence.'

'Doing my job,' Banham replied. 'I want to talk to you, but that will have to wait until I've handled my present investigation.'

'We'll talk here and now!' Determination edged the sheriff's tone. 'I got word early this morning that one of Dolan's riders was killed in the night and his horse was stolen. That horse you just rode in on looks like it's got the Big D brand on it. Tell me about it.'

Banham looked at the sheriff. Bain was braced for trouble, his right hand by his side, fingers splayed for a fast draw, and he wondered what was in the local lawman's mind. He shifted his gaze, and caught furtive movement from an alley mouth to the sheriff's left. The brim of a sombrero poked out, and Banham saw Lopez's dark face beneath it. The Mexican deputy was watching him, gun in his hand, and Banham spoke in a clipped tone.

'Sheriff, if Lopez is covering me while you tackle me then you'd better change your ideas pretty damn quick. I'll shoot without warning anyone who points a gun at me.'

Bain bristled, his gaze turning bleak. He inhaled deeply, held the breath for a few moments, and then exhaled sharply.

'Now see here, Banham. I'm the sheriff of this county, and no penny-ante marshal is gonna come in here and try to run rings around me. Just stand right where you are and answer my questions.'

'Go back to your office and wait there until I come to you,' Banham rapped. 'And while you're waiting for me I suggest you look through your recent mail and see what you've got from my head office. It should tell you I'm coming on a visit, and how you should handle me. Now get out of here. I've got to do what I'm here for – and take that skulking deputy with you before he gets a slug where he can't digest it.'

Bain gave all the signs of wanting to disobey, and stood rooted to the spot for several tense seconds before turning away and heading back the way he had come. He called to Lopez as he passed the alley, and the Mexican deputy emerged from cover and accompanied Bain along the street.

Banham turned his attention to Lola's horse, assuming that she was in the banker's house. He went to the door and knocked. After a short wait, he heard the door being unlocked. When it was opened he looked into the face of a young woman, who smiled, although he could not recollect seeing her before.

'Marshal Banham,' she said. 'I remember you from your visit to the town five years ago, and Lola talked about you when she arrived early this morning. I'm Rachel Simpson. My father runs the bank. Come in, please. I expect you want to talk to Lola.'

She stepped back a pace, pulling the door wider, and Banham removed his hat and stepped over the threshold. She closed the door behind him and led the way into a big sitting room, where Lola was seated in a comfortable upholstered chair in a position that gave her an unrestricted view of the street outside the house. Banham suppressed a sigh. She had been watching him outside with the sheriff, and he wondered what was in her mind.

'So here you are,' Lola smiled, although her eyes were unfriendly.

'I spent the early morning following your horse tracks. The last I saw of you in the night you had three gunmen around you who looked as if they were going to drag you back to Dolan.'

'I was in no danger from them. It was you they were after. I got you off the ranch without trouble, and it was up to you to get yourself away. I heard a lot of shooting.' She grimaced. 'I hope no one was killed.'

'Just tell me what's going on? I told Dolan I'm a lawman, and he set his crew on me.'

'Do you think he's the man responsible for all the trouble around here?' She laughed harshly. 'You couldn't be further from the truth. Someone is out to steal Dolan's ranch, and he was told that a state marshal was coming to arrest him.'

Banham frowned. 'Who told him that?'

'You'll have to go back to the ranch and talk to him to find out.' Lola shrugged. 'But if you did that, I wouldn't take any bets on your success. By now the whole crew will be out looking for you, and if you have killed any of them then you're in bad trouble right now.'

'You've changed your attitude to me since last night,' he accused.

'Last night was different. If Dolan had killed you when you showed up he would have thrown away any chance of beating the set-up against him. Now you're alive and ready to get after the bad men there's a chance you'll be able to clear Dolan.'

Banham grimaced. 'I've started an initial investigation and we'll see what turns up. How long will you be staying in town?'

Lola smiled. 'I'll be here for at least a week. But I don't want to see you during that time. It will be too dangerous for you and I don't want to be dragged into any situation that could give Dolan a reason to get at me. Life is not good as it is, so stay away from me. Whatever we had going between us five years ago is over and done with. As far as I'm concerned it never happened. If I want to talk to you then I'll find a way of getting in touch.'

'If I need to talk to you then I'll call here, and you better be ready to see me,' Banham said harshly. 'Don't try to give me the run-around, Lola.'

She pulled a face and her lips twisted, but she remained silent. He gazed at her for some moments, trying to read what was behind her attitude, but her face was giving nothing away and he turned to depart.

As he left the house, Lola said, 'Try your luck with Ace Connell. He's a gambler in Murphy's saloon, and he's always more than ready to make extra dough from his contacts.'

Banham did not pause and left the house. He checked his surroundings as he walked along the sidewalk to a saloon with a large board over the doorway advertising Murphy's wares. Three horses were hitched to a rail in front of the batwings, and Banham stiffened for action when he saw Dolan's Big D brand on their left flanks. A cowpoke was standing by the batwings, and he turned his attention to the interior of the saloon when Banham made to enter.

Banham's spurs tinkled on the boardwalk as he reached out to thrust open the batwings with his left hand, and the cowpoke turned to face him, a pistol grasped in his right hand.

Seeing the weapon, Banham seized the man's left

arm and exerted pressure, his gaze on the gun the man was holding. He crowded forward and used his weight and strength to propel the cowpoke into the saloon. The man yelled and began to resist. Banham stuck out his right hand, caught hold of the pistol that was swinging to cover him, and wrenched it from the man's grasp. He swung the gun in a fast arc and slammed the barrel back-handed against the right side of the man's head. They were crossing the threshold of the saloon at that moment, and the cowpoke fell to his knees and then sprawled on his face on the pine boards. Banham tossed the man's gun into a corner.

Banham's gaze was already sweeping the interior. He saw at a glance the long bar running the whole length of the right-hand wall. A bartender wearing a white apron over his clothes was behind the bar, talking with two cowpokes drinking beer, but looking towards the batwings. The cowpoke on the right dropped his half-empty glass and reached for his holstered gun, moving away from the bar as Banham set his gun hand streaking to his pistol. The bartender ducked below the level of the bar and remained out of sight. Banham could see the second cowpoke reaching for his holstered pistol.

Banham fired two quick shots. The cowpoke on the right dropped his pistol and followed it down to the floor. The second cowpoke brought his gun into play, but he was hurrying, and his first slug bored through the batwings. Banham fired another shot that buried itself in the man's chest. He went down clawing thin air. Banham faced the bar.

'Hey, barkeep,' he called. 'Get up so I can see you, and make sure you ain't holding a gun.'

'I ain't mixed up in anything,' the man replied. 'I'm taking cover, that's all.'

'Get up slowly. The shooting is over now.' Banham ran his eyes over the saloon. There were several men present, but none showed interest in the shooting.

The bartender got to his feet and stood behind the bar with his hands raised shoulder high. He looked at the two fallen cowpokes. One was dead, with that particular stillness that accompanied death. The other was also still but his eyelids were flickering. The silence pervading the big room was heavy. Banham could hear voices out on the street querying the disturbance, and then heavy feet pounded the sidewalk. The batwings were thrust open, and Sheriff Bain appeared, followed by his Mexican deputy.

The sheriff stopped in mid-stride and looked around. He was holding a pistol in his right hand. Lopez was clutching a sawn-off shot-gun.

'I guessed you would be mixed up in this,' Bain growled. 'So what's going on?'

'Three cowpokes turned hostile when I came into the saloon,' Banham responded. 'The man sleeping on the floor tried to overpower me as I entered. The other two drew guns and started shooting as soon as they saw me. I'm about to ask questions, but you can take over here and do that while I pursue other lines of enquiry. These men are riders for Dolan, so I suggest you start looking in that direction. Better than that, you can clean up the mess in here and then go out to the Big D ranch and arrest Dolan. I want him for questioning.'

'I ain't here to do your dirty work,' Bain growled. 'I'm gonna ask my own questions, and if I don't get the answers I want then I'll arrest you on a charge of suspected murder and throw you in a cell.'

Banham walked forward to confront the sheriff, and was aware that the shot-gun Lopez was holding covered his movements. He faced the sheriff and gazed into Bain's eyes.

'Did I hear you right?' Banham demanded. 'Are you so ignorant of the law that you don't know how to act?'

'I'm the legally elected sheriff of this county, and nobody can give me orders. You say you're a deputy marshal, but I ain't got no proof of that, and no one is gonna pull the wool over my eyes. I'll talk to Virgil Swanston, the lawyer, about the workings of the law, and he'll set me right. In the meantime you can stop giving your orders as if you own the place and let me get on with my duty. Lopez, keep your gun on our Mr Deputy Marshal, and you know what to do if he gives you any trouble.'

Banham moved so fast when he drew his Colt that Bain, already holding his pistol in his right hand, had no time to blink before Banham's gun was prodding him painfully in the chest. He heard Lopez ear back the hammers of the shot-gun and

44

moved around the sheriff until the blocky lawman was between him and the Mexican.

'Lopez, you better ease your hammers and put down the gun before it hurts someone. Do it now.'

Banham waited for Lopez to comply, but the Mexican stood his ground.

'What shall I do, Sheriff?' he asked.

'You better do like he says,' Bain replied through clenched teeth. He relaxed the fingers of his right hand and his pistol fell to the floor. 'Now what do you want?' he demanded.

'If you don't plan to cooperate with me then you'd better get out of here, and stay out. If you cross my tracks again I'll throw you and the Mex in jail.'

'I ain't done anything wrong,' Bain protested. 'Pull in your horns before I get good and angry. I won't stand by and watch you make a fool of me in front of the townsfolk.'

'You're doing the fooling. Go on and get out of here.' Banham stepped back from Bain and levelled his pistol at Lopez. 'That goes for you, too.'

The Mexican held his pose for several moments, indecision showing in his dark eyes. Then he laid aside the shot-gun and turned and walked to the batwings. Bain followed him, and the two local lawmen departed, leaving the swing doors moving restlessly. Banham stood motionless until the sound of departing footsteps faded. He went to the alley door and stepped out into the encroaching darkness.

The chatter of excited voices came to his ears from the street in front of the saloon. He walked to the alley mouth and peered out, saw a group of several men standing in the dusty street and noted Bain and Lopez standing with them. The sheriff was in the act of borrowing a pistol from one of the bystanders.

'Sheriff, get rid of that gun,' Banham called. 'If I see you armed again I'll shoot you dead. Now get off the street. This is your last warning.'

Bain threw down the gun as if it had suddenly become too hot to hold. He looked around until he spotted Banham's grim figure on the sidewalk in the alley mouth and turned instantly to head for the law office with Lopez following him. Banham sighed long and heavily as he watched them depart. When they vanished into the dense shadows along the street, he turned away, intent on making some progress in the enigma facing him.

He needed to see his sister, Hannah, and returned to the alley beside the saloon. He walked into the black wall of darkness, paused for several moments for his eyes to become accustomed to the night, and then made his way to the back lot, right hand close to the butt of his holstered gun and his ears strained for hostile sound. The darkness closed around him like a heavy curtain. He peered around the back lots, and finally walked along behind the buildings fronting Main Street, heading for the general store.

As he passed the mouth of the alley between the

bank and the store he heard the sound of a stone turning under a hesitant foot. His pistol rasped out of leather and he bent almost double as he changed position in case someone was covering him. He heard a gasp, and a straying ray of lamp light from the rear of the store revealed a slight figure emerging from the alley. He stepped forward quickly, reached out with his left hand, and secured a grip on the rifle being carried by the newcomer.

A startled gasp escaped Aggie as she was dragged into Banham's arms. He caught the tang of her perfume, which had been tantalising his nostrils since he'd met her at the ranch, and he didn't know whether to be angry or pleased at their meeting. He took the rifle from her hands despite her struggle to resist, pressed his mouth close to her left ear and spoke hoarsely.

'Stop fighting me and stay quiet,' he hissed. 'What are you doing out here, sneaking around with a rifle? Don't you know that any man coming upon you, armed and prowling, would shoot you down without hesitation?'

'Dale, I'm so glad I bumped into you,' Aggie replied. 'We heard the shooting and I thought you were in trouble so I came out to back you up. You'll find precious little help around here from anybody else.'

'I wasn't in trouble, Aggie.'

'Oh.' She sounded disappointed. 'Are you angry with me?'

'I'm not pleased that you placed yourself in

danger. I might have shot you in the darkness. This is not a game I'm playing, and the sooner you realize that the better. I was on my way to the store to see you and Hannah. You could help me a lot, but not by trying to back me with a gun.'

'I'm sorry,' she said contritely. 'I won't do it again.'

He held her rifle in his left hand, and when she blundered in the shadows he reached out and caught hold of her elbow before she could fall. She leaned against him momentarily and he supported her for some moments before she recovered her equilibrium and moved away. He followed her along the back lots towards the store, and just when he thought there was no further danger a harsh voice cut through the silence.

'Stand where you are! Lift your hands, and don't reach for your guns. I've got you covered.'

Banham moved instinctively, grasping Aggie in his left arm and hurling himself to his left, taking her with him, bracing himself for an impact with the ground. He reached for his pistol as a gun flash split the shadows, and a number of shots hammered through the silence. He rolled across Aggie to protect her from the shooting and triggered his pistol, aiming for gun flashes. . . .

FOUR

The shooting was sustained for only a few moments, and silence fell when complete darkness returned. Banham strained his ears for hostile sound, but fading echoes blotted out everything around him, and he waited with gun uplifted until the night regained its peacefulness. Then he turned to Aggie, who had remained silent and still by his side and, when she did not reply to his demand to know if she was well, he bent over her, shaking her shoulder.

'Aggie, are you OK?' he repeated, and shook her again when there was no answer. It was too dark for him to see her, and concern caught him as he feared she had been hit by a bullet. He glanced around again and decided the attacker had gone. He took a match out of his hatband and struck it, holding its feeble flame close to her, and when he saw an ominous stain of blood at her right hip he was galvanised into action.

He got up and bent to slide his arms around her, lifted her bodily, and hurried through the shadows to the rear of the store. There was a lighted window that gave a view of the back lots, and he glanced into the room and saw his sister Hannah seated inside in the company of an older man and woman. He eased Aggie on to his left shoulder and knocked on the window. Hannah looked towards him and he thrust his face against the glass. When Hannah saw him her expression changed quickly, and she came running to open the back door.

Banham carried Aggie gently into the room and eased her down on a couch. Hannah pushed him aside and bent over her friend. Banham watched silently as his sister revealed Aggie's wound, and he sighed in relief when he judged the damage was not too bad.

The man came close and looked down. 'I'd better get Doc Palmer,' he said. Banham looked at him and the man nodded. 'I'm Ned Browning, Aggie's father,' he said, and left the room.

'What happened?' Hannah demanded. She turned to the older woman, who was stiff in shock. 'Would you get some water and clean cloth, Mrs Browning?'

Mrs Browning nodded and went out. Hannah looked at Banham. He heaved a sigh.

'I bumped into Aggie after my trouble in the saloon,' he said. 'She was prowling around in the dark with her rifle.' He went on to explain the ensuing incidents.

Ned Browning returned with the doctor, a good-looking young man, tall and lean, with blond hair and blues eyes. Hannah introduced Banham and the doctor held out his hand.

'Glad to know you, Marshal,' Palmer said as he turned his attention to Aggie. 'It's about time we got some law and order around here.'

Hannah led Banham out to the kitchen, where food was cooking on a stove.

'I guess you must be hungry, Dale. I had no idea when you'd show up again, so I've kept a meal simmering for you ever since we got here. What have you been doing since you left us?'

'Dolan turned his outfit on me and I've been dodging them, shooting some when I had to. But that's not the way to handle this business. I want you to fill me in with some facts about what's been going on around here during the past five years and I'll make my own luck before somebody tries his hand at killing me.'

'I'll help you if I can,' Hannah shook her head dubiously as she spoke. 'But I don't think I know anything that would help you.'

'Let's start with a few names. I particularly want to meet up again with Ed Harmon. I caught him with some of the local bad men five years ago. Is he still around?'

'He's the town drunk now, and he's down that trail just about as far as he can get. Since his wife kicked him out of their home he hasn't done a stroke of work, and spends all his waking hours drinking.'

'Where does he bed down?'

'This time of year he'll sleep where he falls down. In the winter Charlie Strawhorn lets him use the loft in the livery barn. Harmon is not in good shape these days, and I'll be surprised if he proves to be of any use to you. Sit down at the table and I'll dish up some food.'

Banham sat down, and ate ravenously of the food Hannah placed before him. She sat opposite him, talking generally about local problems until he had finished satisfying his hunger. He leaned back in his seat and sighed in satisfaction.

'I'd better get back to Aggie,' Hannah said at length. 'The doctor will have finished with her by now. If you're going after Harmon then be very careful. He's still a dangerous man.'

'I'll get along now.' Banham got to his feet. 'I'll be busy for several days, I should think. But I know where to find you, and I'll drop in to see you when I can. Don't go wandering around the town until I've got a good hold on the tail of this trouble.'

She kissed him on the chin and turned away, and Banham went out to the sidewalk and immediately lost himself in the shadows. He walked to the edge of town where the livery barn was situated. The place was dark, silent and still, with only a solitary lantern hanging over the half-open front door. He approached cautiously, his gun in his right hand. He entered the barn and halted with his back to the door, his keen gaze surveying the shadows inside.

A figure took shape out of denser shadows and confronted him.

'Are you the stable man?' Banham asked.

'I'm Charlie Strawhorn. I own this place. What are you doing here in the dark? Do you reckon to steal a horse?'

'I'm a lawman, and I need to speak with Ed Harmon. Is he around?'

'I expect he's bedded down in my loft, and if he is he won't be in any fit state to talk. Why do you want him? Has he broken the law?'

'I thought he gave up breaking the law when I arrested him five years ago. I hear he can't hold down a job these days, so I'm wondering where he gets his dough from.'

Strawhorn laughed. 'That's a leading question around here. A lot of men can't give you a straight answer to that. I give Harmon some dough for keeping an eye on this place when he's sober enough to stand up, but he's worse now than he was even a year ago. Take the lantern out of my office and go up to the loft. If you can't see Harmon you'll certainly hear him snoring.'

Banham went into the small office and picked up the lantern. He went to the ladder that gave access to the loft, holding the light in his left hand. He heard the sound of snoring when he reached the top of the ladder and found Ed Harmon stretched out on a pile of straw. There was the smell of whiskey emanating from the man's gaping mouth.

Harmon was short and slight, his face sprouting greying hair. Banham kicked the upturned boot on Harmon's right foot. There was no reaction. Banham kicked harder. Harmon did not stir. It was obvious that he would not regain his senses at least until the sun showed in the morning.

For a few moments Banham stood looking down at the drunken man. He heard a sound below the ladder, and saw Strawhorn climbing up to the loft with a pail of water in one hand.

'I've always wanted to do this to Harmon,' he said, upending the bucket and spilling a stream of water into the sleeping man's upturned face.

Harmon stopped snoring. He sat up with a violent motion, gasping and spraying water. He uttered a yell and came up off the straw as if his feet had springs attached. He lunged unsteadily at Banham, his hands clenched into fists. Banham, encumbered with the lantern, threw a right-hand punch that caught Harmon on the jaw, and Harmon went down like a falling log. Banham bent over him and jerked a pistol out of his waistband.

'I guess I'll come back to him in the morning.' Banham took Harmon's pistol and stuck it in his belt.

They descended the ladder and Banham departed, mindful of the fact that Dolan's outfit were intent on killing him. He stayed in the shadows, made his way to Murphy's saloon, and peered over the batwings, looking for any face he could recall from his past. A score of men were in the saloon, and he noted some cowpokes among them but did not recognize anyone.

Sheriff Bain was at the bar, talking seriously with a smartly dressed man wearing a brown suit, a stiff collar and a grey bow tie. Pat Murphy. Banham nodded. He could do worse than talk to the saloon man. He pushed through the batwings and crossed to the bar. Silence came when he was seen, and a moment later a man arose from a chair at one of the gaming tables and came towards Banham, intention showing plainly on his rugged face. He was dressed in range clothes and had a six-gun on his right hip.

Banham paused and waited. The man approached to within ten feet and halted. His right hand was down at his side, fingers resting on the butt of the pistol holstered there. He gazed at Banham, his stark eyes filled with concentration. When he spoke his lips moved stiffly, as if he had lost control of his physical power.

'You're Banham, the lawman, huh?' he demanded.

'Who are you?' Banham countered.

'Deke Bascombe. You killed a friend of mine over Trailville way a couple of years ago. I've been looking for you, Banham. Reach for your gun.'

Banham drew his gun instantly with the speed of a striking snake. Bascombe set his hand in motion and palmed his Colt but stopped his draw before it was half completed for he was looking into the muzzle of Banham's gun, which was cocked and ready for action. A sigh escaped Bascombe as he opened his fingers, and there was a dull thud when his gun hit the floor.

The silence in the saloon was overwhelming. Tension clutched at Banham's throat. He glimpsed Sheriff Bain pushing himself away from the bar, and Bain walked towards the side door, intent on leaving, his face harshly set, his boots thudding on the floor.

'Sheriff, where in hell are you going?' Banham rapped.

Bain stopped and looked over his shoulder, his expression changing, frowning as if his sense of awareness had suddenly deserted him. There was no other movement in the big room. Bascombe was like a graven image. His pistol lay on the floor, and he was gazing at it as if wondering why he had dropped it, but Banham's gun was covering him with its black eye unwavering, offering violent death.

'It looks to me like you're involved in a private fight,' Bain said glibly. 'I got enough trouble on my plate without barging into every gun scrape that comes along.'

'You'd better back me up. Walk out on me and you're finished for good around here. Bascombe dropped on to me like a hawk the minute I came through the batwings. I want him placed behind bars before I have to kill him. Take him out of here and hold him until I can get around to dealing with him. Jump to it.'

Bain went to his fallen gun and picked it up. He came reluctantly to Bascombe's side; jabbed his gun muzzle in Bascombe's ribs.

'You heard the man,' he snarled. 'Get moving. We all have to jump when a visiting marshal gives an order. Out the door and turn left. You'll see the jail when you come to it. Don't give me any trouble or you'll be lying stiff and cold in Frank Coe's mortuary come morning.'

Bascombe lurched forward into motion under the menace of Bain's gun, and Banham slid his pistol back into its holster as the sheriff and his prisoner departed. The saloon came back to life as the batwings closed behind them. Banham went to the bar and the 'tender moved quickly to place a glass and a bottle of whiskey in front of him. The smartly dressed man that had been talking to Bain turned to Banham with a ready grin on his face, although the expression in his dark eyes was cold as snow.

'I was telling Bain what a helluva job you lawmen really have,' Murphy said with a grin. 'In case you don't know, I'm Murphy and I own this place. I'm glad to see you here, Marshal. The local law is not what it is reputed to be and you'll be greatly appreciated when you start tackling the bad men. Have a drink on the house. I'm all for law and order, and it would please me greatly if I can buy you a drink.'

'Whiskey,' Banham said.

Murphy signalled to the bartender and another glass appeared on the bar before them. Murphy poured two liberal glasses of whiskey and raised his glass to his lips. He gazed at Banham over the rim of his glass.

'Your very good health, Marshal,' he declared. 'I wish you every success in your job. If there is anything I can do to help you then just call on me.'

'There's a lot of trouble around here but no one seems to know who's behind it,' Banham said. 'I reckon, if you put your mind to it, you could name several men who run outside the law.'

'If I knew anything like that I wouldn't be stupid enough to tell you about it,' Murphy replied. 'If I opened my mouth to half of what I know, I'd be dead very quickly. I learned early in life to keep my nose clean and stay out of the bad business around me. Sorry, but I can't help you.' He paused and considered. 'You could talk to Abner Varney. He owns the gun shop. I heard some time ago that he was in with some of the bad men. But don't tell him I gave you his name.'

Banham drank his whiskey, thanked Murphy, and departed. He stood on the sidewalk thinking, then removed his law badge and put it in his pocket. He could feel tiredness tugging at him, and fought against the mental images trying to overpower him. He needed sleep, and plenty of it, but he also needed a breakthrough in this crooked business and he had to keep going until he found one.

There was a light in the gun shop, and a big man was standing behind the counter working on a rifle in his hands. Banham tried the door and found it locked. The man looked up and made a sweeping movement with his right hand.

'I'm closed until eight in the morning,' he shouted. 'Come back then.'

'I want a few words with you,' Banham replied. 'Open the door.'

Abner Varney shrugged and put aside the rifle. He came to the door and unlocked it, scowling, his expression showing impatience. He was wearing a white apron over his clothes. He had a big body that was running to fat, a large fleshy face with piggy eyes, and his double chin sagged as if the black spade beard he was wearing was too heavy for it.

'What the hell do you want?' he demanded. 'Can't it wait until tomorrow?'

'I've just got into town,' Banham replied. 'A man told me to look you up if I wanted a good job.'

'What man?' Suspicion filled Varney's dark eyes.

'I can't tell you that. He was anxious to remain unknown. You know him well, and he knows all about your business.'

'You're talking in riddles, mister. I never set eyes on you before, and I never do business with anyone I don't know. You're wasting my time so get lost.'

Varney started to close the door and Banham stepped forward, pushing his foot over the step to prevent the door closing. Varney cursed and stepped back, dropping his hand to the butt of his holstered gun.

'I was told you can find jobs for men who are handy with a gun,' Banham said.

Varney took his hand away from his gun and went

back to the counter. Banham stepped into the shop and closed the door. Varney turned to face him. His expression had changed. He was smiling now.

'You're riding the owl hoot trail, huh?' he demanded.

'Not any more. Can you fix me up?'

'What's your handle?'

'I don't use a name. I come from Houston, and if that's good enough for Sam Houston then it is good enough for me.'

'OK, Houston. What have you done on your back trail? Who have you worked with?'

'Dan Poggin and his crooked bunch, and some of the gangs along the border, doing anything from running wetbacks to killing for dough.'

'Poggin got shot up along the Brazos.'

'That's why I'm on the loose now,' Banham said. 'I need some eating money so I'm willing to do anything. I heard a week ago that things were jumping on this range, so here I am, rarin' to go.'

'There is a gang running things around here, and they're allus on the look-out for good men. Go out to Dolan's spread and talk to his ramrod, Jake Dillman. He'll see you right. If you need some eating money until you get hired I'll lend you ten dollars.'

'Thanks. I got enough dough so long as I can pick up a job pretty damn quick. I'm mighty beholden to you, Varney.'

'You can buy your cartridges from me, and pick your needs from anything else I got on my shelves.

60

That'll keep us straight.'

'I'll take a coupla boxes of .45s right now.' Banham took a thin roll of green backs from his pocket, peeled off a single note and handed it to Varney. 'Keep the change.'

Varney produced two boxes of cartridges and took Banham's money.

'You'll need to go out to Big D to see Dillman. I've got a man living opposite who'll show you the way. It's part of his job. I'll tell him to saddle up and meet you in front of Murphy's saloon in twenty minutes.'

'I'm on my way!' Banham left the shop and paused in the shadows of an alley. Varney emerged from the shop within a few minutes, crossed the street and entered an opposite alley. A few minutes later he reappeared and went back to his shop.

Banham went along the street to the stable and prepared his horse, the Big D mount he had taken from the scene of the fight on Dolan's range. They had killed his horse and he was content to use one of their animals. A man entered the stable, saddled a horse in the shadows, and departed quickly. Banham followed him, and when the man halted in front of Murphy's saloon, Banham rode to his side.

'Is your name Houston?' the stranger demanded.

'That's me,' Banham replied.

'I'm Charlie Moss. I got word to show you the way to Dillman out at Dolan's place.'

'Lead on.'

Moss swung his horse and used his spurs. The animal jumped into motion and hit the trail for out of town. Banham followed at a steady pace, and a mile out on the trail Moss was sitting on his horse, waiting for him; Banham could not make out the details of the man's face, the night was so dense.

'I thought you said you wanted to get out to Dolan's spread,' Moss said.

'Not at your pace,' Banham replied.

'I ain't got all night,' Moss rasped. He set off again at an easier pace.

Banham remained at Moss's side. He was biding his time. He could not turn up to see Dillman posing as Houston because he was known to the outfit as a lawman. He hoped to get Moss talking about himself, what he was doing working for Varney. But Moss was close-mouthed and did not seem likely to offer anything about himself. Banham finally came to the conclusion that he was wasting his time and reined in and drew his gun.

'What gives?' Moss asked.

'I ain't ready to see Dillman yet, so you're wasting your time. Head back to town and tell Varney I'll look up Dillman tomorrow.'

'If you ride into Dolan's spread aione you're likely to wind with a slug in you.'

'I'll take that chance.'

'It'll be your funeral.' Moss jerked on his reins, turned his horse, and rode back to town.

Banham waited until the sounds of Moss's exit faded into the night before he moved on. His eyes were now accustomed to the dark range, and he watched his surroundings as he continued to Dolan's ranch. The night was perfect for his nocturnal activities, no moon and a clear sky. He saw and heard nothing as he approached the sleeping ranch, but he was not deceived by the silence. He reined up in the shadow of a barn, secured his horse, ensured that he had a plentiful supply of cartridges, then moved in on foot to take observations of the cow spread.

He sought out the foreman's shack, which was standing to one side of a large corral and within easy walking distance of the cook shack. He noticed a rent in the sacking being used as a curtain in the window in Dillman's quarters and sneaked in to apply his right eye to the small aperture. Dillman was seated at a table inside, with four other men, playing poker.

A slight sound in the shadows to Banham's right had him moving swiftly away from the window and reaching for the butt of his gun, but a hand came out of the night, grasped his gun hand, and he heard the click of a pistol being cocked and then the muzzle of the weapon was pressed against the side of his head.

'Stay quiet and peaceful if you want to see sun up,' a harsh voice whispered in his ear.

Banham froze, recognizing Dolan's voice. A hand snatched his six-gun.

'You've got sense, Marshal,' Dolan said. 'I don't want to disturb Dillman right now. Let's go over to the ranch house and we'll do some talking, and don't make a sound if you want to keep breathing.'

FIVE

Banham had no option but to obey, and moved in the direction of the ranch headquarters, aware that at least two other men were with Dolan. They crossed the yard and moved on to the porch. Dolan entered the house and lit a lamp, and Banham was invited in. Guns covered him as he faced Dolan, who was grim-faced.

'I figured you'd be back,' Dolan said, 'and here you are, turning up like a bad penny.'

'What's on your mind?' Banham asked.

'What were you planning to do?' Dolan countered. 'Did you come back to see me or Dillman?'

'Dillman,' Banham admitted.

'Dillman and not me?' Dolan persisted. 'Who told you to see Dillman?'

'I met a man in town. Now tell me what's going on here?'

'I know what you're thinking about this set-up, but you're wrong. This is my ranch and I run it my way, but Dillman has a gang of hard cases backing him and they are running the bad business. The men who followed you from here earlier are not working for me, and they have a bear's grip on the situation. They have a hold on me which I can't break, and there would be a killing spree right here if I stepped out of line. My hands are tied, and I've given up trying to break Dillman's hold on the situation. He's got me covered all ways to the middle.'

Banham shook his head. 'No man could have such a hold on another man. A bullet is a great leveller. Sam Colt made all men equal.'

'Go for Dillman now and arrest him and then I might have a dog's chance.' Dolan put out a hand and grasped Banham's left sleeve. 'Did you leave Lola safe in town?'

'She's OK. Am I right in thinking there is more than Lola's health at risk?'

'My daughter Julie is under threat from Dillman. If I step out of line then she will be killed.'

'Where is she now? I didn't see her here when I was around earlier.'

'She's in Austin, getting a good education. Dillman has someone near her in Austin. I daren't take a chance on the odds of getting her clear. So I have to eat crow and stay put.'

'If you're telling the truth then give me your daughter's address in Austin and I'll arrange for some good men to take care of her. Dillman's gunman wouldn't have a chance, and as soon as I get word that your daughter is safe we could move in on the bad men.'

'I'm afraid to take a chance with my daughter's life.' Dolan shook his head, 'and it would be a waste of your time trying to persuade me to change my mind.'

'You should ride to Austin and take your daughter out of there. I'll keep an eye on this place until I hear from you that all is well, and then I'll move in against Dillman. What could be simpler than that?'

'I don't know. Lawmen have a way of talking, and they don't pick up the bill if things go wrong. I'll have to let me think about it.'

'Don't take too long.'

'Time wouldn't matter so much if you arrested Dillman now and threw him in the hoosegow.'

'Have you got a specific charge against him?'

'Sure I have. Robbery will do for a start, and he tried to have you killed earlier.'

Banham looked into Dolan's eyes and wondered if the rancher was telling the truth. He decided to go along with Dolan's idea, and when he said so Dolan snapped into action. He sent one of his men to saddle horses and take them just clear of the ranch on the trail to town.

'Let me get clear of the ranch before you take Dillman,' Dolan said.

'Where are you going?'

'I'll raise a little hell of my own and knock Dillman back a few paces. There's a gun seller in town who could have a big hand in what's going on around here and I need to get a good look at him. But I'll be watching you, Marshal. When you get

Dillman in jail, and prove that you can keep him there, we'll get together and clean out this robbers' roost.'

Dolan turned and departed, leaving Banham standing in the ranch house. Banham wondered what he had let himself in for, but he was prepared to go along with Dolan because he wanted Dillman behind bars in order to get his investigation under way. He went out to the porch and stood in the shadows, looking around the spread. There was lamplight in the bunkhouse and a glimmer at the small window in Dillman's shack. Silence hung like a wet blanket over the ranch, and Banham instinctively geared himself for action.

When he thought he'd given Dolan enough time to get clear of the ranch he drew his pistol and checked the loads in the cylinder. He stepped off the porch and crossed to the foreman's shack, his gun ready in his hand. He gained the side wall of the little building and flattened himself in the denser shadows before glancing through the window. Dillman and the four men were still playing cards. He drew a deep breath to steady himself, and then reached for the handle of the door with his left hand.

Banham opened the door and stepped into the shack. He covered the five men, who looked up at him in shock. Dillman sat very still when he saw Banham's gun, and a hard glitter came into his eyes. The other four men froze and became watchful.

'What do you want?' Dillman demanded.

'I want you,' Banham replied. 'You set some gunmen on my trail, and I want to talk to you about that, and several other things that have happened on this range.'

'I ain't going anywhere with anyone.' Dillman leaned back in his seat and grinned. 'You made a big mistake, walking in here alone. You won't find it so easy to leave this time.'

'Aren't you overlooking my gun?' Banham waggled the weapon.

'You're a tin pot lawman,' said the man on Dillman's right. He was a hard case with cold eyes, slim and tense like a prairie wolf. He was wearing town clothes, and looked as if he had never seen a cow on the range. 'You're the kind that's not worth more than ten for a nickel.'

'Cut the hot air,' Banham said. 'One at a time, all of you get rid of your hardware, starting with you, mister,' he told the man who had challenged him.

'Do like he says, Jed,' Dillman rapped.

'Like hell! No badge-toter can come in here and tell me what to do.'

Banham thumbed back his hammer. The muzzle of his gun flipped in Jed's direction, and the silence and tension vanished in smoke and flame when Banham squeezed his trigger. Jed went over backwards from the table, blood spouting from his throat, and his gun, which he had managed to draw, slipped out of his nerveless hand.

Dillman grasped the edge of the table and lifted it powerfully, shoving it forward, and the other men around it were scattered like logs caught up in a flood surge. Banham fired again, his slug clipping the top edge of the table and smashing into Dillman's right shoulder. Dillman fell to his right, striking the floor with his face, and he stayed down. Banham changed his position, moving to his right, and saw one of the surviving card players trying, with desperate haste, to bring his gun into action. Banham's gun blasted again. The man fell back, and blood ran from his gaping mouth in a red gush.

Banham cocked his gun. The remaining two men came up from the floor side by side, guns smoking. Banham fired. The nearest man toppled over as the slug thudded into his chest, broke two ribs before piercing his heart. The last man was already levelling his gun. Banham shaded him, fired first, and a torrent of blood erupted from his adversary's mouth as the slug tore out his throat.

Banham braced his legs, his breathing steady. He surveyed the result of the action and heaved a sigh, his thoughts surging ahead. Now all he had to do was get Dillman out of here and into the cells in town.

A harsh voice called from the darkness outside the shack, and Banham reloaded his gun.

'Hey, Dillman, what in hell is going on in there?'

Banham spun the cylinder and his right index finger pressed lightly against the curved metal of the trigger. He did not reply to the question, but moved around the shack, checking the downed men. Three were dead, and Dillman and another were still breathing. Dillman was conscious. His eyes were open, fixed on Banham in an unblinking gaze.

'You won't get away from here,' Dillman muttered.

'We're leaving immediately, and don't give me any trouble or I'll leave you dead.'

'You can't move me. I've been shot in the body and I'm like to die if I'm moved. Get the doctor out here but quick.'

'You're hit in the shoulder, and you'd better get on your feet or I'll kick you up. Moments ago you were trying to kill me, so don't expect any favours from me. Get up and start moving.'

Dillman did not move. Banham bent over him, dragged him to his feet, and pushed him roughly toward the door.

'When we get outside I don't want to hear a sound from you,' Banham continued. 'One whisper and I'll gut-shoot you.'

Dillman sagged against Banham, and tried to snatch Banham's pistol out of his hand. Banham slammed the barrel in a back-handed movement into Dillman's face. Dillman dropped to the ground. Banham grasped his collar and hauled him outside into the night. Someone was shouting in the distance, evidently alerting the rest of the crew. Banham dragged Dillman away from the shack, heading for the spot where he had left his horse.

There were no further incidents on the ranch. Banham reached his horse and threw Dillman across the saddle, ignoring the man's protests about

71

rough treatment. Mounting behind his prisoner, he set off towards town, ears pitched for sounds of pursuit. When he was well clear of the ranch, he stopped and took a set of handcuffs from a saddle-bag, put them around Dillman's wrists and secured them with a latigo to the back of his saddle. He mounted the horse behind Dillman and continued to town, eventually joining the main trail.

When he could see the lights of the town, he increased his pace. Dillman was silent now. Banham suddenly reined in. He could hear the sound of voices just ahead, but could see nothing. Then he recognized the sheriff's voice, and a moment later the Mexican deputy replied.

'Why do you want to sit out here half the night looking at the stars, Sheriff?'

'I'm not looking at the stars, you half-baked Mexican, I got a tip-off earlier that someone I particularly want to catch will be coming into town this evening, and with a little luck he'll show up and we'll grab him. Now keep quiet. The way you talk, I reckon they can hear you as far as Dolan's place.'

Banham kneed his horse and the animal moved forward obediently.

'Hey, Sheriff, this is Marshal Banham. I'm coming in with Dillman.'

'Have you been out to Dolan's place again?' Bain demanded.

'Sure. That's where all the action is. There was a shoot-out when I tried to arrest Dillman.'

'And you're still breathing?' Lopez sneered.

Banham halted his horse nose to nose with the sheriff's animal. Bain was gripping a pistol in his right hand. His face was shadowed by his Stetson.

'Get off your horse and check Dillman, Lopez,' Bain said.

'Stay where you are, Lopez, Dillman is fit to talk, and he should have some very interesting things to tell me. I don't want you or the sheriff getting anywhere near him. Is that clear?'

'You want to put your prisoner in my jail but bar me from talking to him?'

'That's the general idea, Sheriff. You can feed him, have the doctor in to dress his wound, and handle all his wants. But you better steer clear of talking to him about why he's under arrest.'

'I'll talk to the lawyer about law dealing,' Bain said.

'You can talk to anyone but my prisoner,' Banham replied. 'Now put him in your jail and get the doctor to attend him. I'll be along shortly to check him out.'

'What charge do I hold him on?'

'Attempting to kill a lawman! That will hold him, and the first thing you do when you get to your office is write a report about meeting me here and taking Dillman in charge. Now get moving.'

Bain ordered Lopez to take Dillman to the jail, and followed the Mexican deputy when the horse carrying him was led away. Banham watched them go and then went along the street to the gunsmith's store. He had some unfinished business with Abner Varney.

The gun shop was in darkness, but a light in a back room was clear and bright.

Banham dismounted in an alley and left his horse with trailing reins in a back yard, and as he went to Varney's back door a quiet voice spoke from the nearby shadows.

'Hold it right there, mister, and declare your business. What are you up to at this time of the day?'

'I'm Houston. You're Charlie Moss.' Banham recognized the voice. 'You took me out to Big D earlier.'

'So what are you doing here?'

'I need to talk to Varney. Why are you skulking around in the dark?'

'It's all part of my job. I'm on call day and night for Varney. He's had trouble from a couple of hard cases, and I'm standing by in case he needs help.'

'Stand still, you two, and don't reach for your guns.'

The harsh voice came from the shadows behind Banham, and he heard the sound of boots scraping the hard ground as unseen men came forward from close by. He also heard the ominous sound of guns being cocked, and remained motionless, eyes on Charlie Moss as several figures appeared from the shadows to surround them.

'Dolan,' Banham said, recognizing the rancher's voice. 'What are you doing here? It's not legal for armed men to be prowling around with drawn guns and challenging citizens.'

'I'm out to remove some of the undesirables

74

from town,' Dolan laughed. 'You gave me the idea when we talked earlier, and one of the guys who's gonna get the order to leave is Abel Varney. He's a bad man, and we'll string him up to the nearest tree if he doesn't take notice of what I say. What are you doing here, anyway? Are you looking for Varney?'

'I need to talk to him. And I'll warn you now that the law doesn't take kindly to men who decide to take unlawful action. We have lawmen to handle the bad men, so put up your gun and head back to your ranch and take your men with you.'

'I heard a lot of shooting on my spread as I left it.' Dolan's face was just a blur in the shadows, but suppressed excitement sounded in his rough tone. 'What did you do about Dillman?'

'I had to shoot him before I could arrest him but now he's safe behind bars.'

'Can you hold him?'

'He'll stay where he is until I'm satisfied about him, one way or another. Now take my advice and get out of town. If you know something about Varney that I should know about then come to the law office and make a statement.'

'I'll think over what you say. But I'm gonna talk to Varney right now.'

'If you persist in that attitude I'll be compelled to put you in a cell,' Banham warned.

Dolan laughed and turned away. Banham watched him go to the gun shop door and hammer on it with the butt of his pistol. There were no lights in the front shop, and Dolan soon lost his patience.

He stepped back and kicked the door until the lock broke, and then shouldered his way inside.

Banham started forward but the man who was accompanying Dolan jabbed the muzzle of his gun against Banham's belly.

'Do yourself a favour and go lock yourself in your jail,' he growled.

'I'll lock you all in a cell if you give me any trouble,' Banham warned. 'Put your guns away, and get out of here with your men, Dolan. I won't tell you again.'

His fingers caressed the butt of his holstered gun. He could hear Dolan searching in the private rooms at the back of the shop. Yellow light flared when Dolan found a lamp. Banham waited tensely, and was relieved when Dolan reappeared in the shop doorway.

'He ain't home,' Dolan said. He glanced at his men. 'You three, look through the town, and call me if you see him. I want action now I've made the effort to clean up around here.'

His men departed, and Banham eased his pistol in its holster.

'Are you gonna give me a hand to clean up?' Dolan demanded.

'The only way you can clean up is by giving me information about local men who have broken the law. Come along to the law office, make a statement, and I'll take care of the rest.'

'I won't do that.' Dolan spoke determinedly. 'I know the men causing the trouble, and I want the satisfaction of stopping them. I've got my daughter's life to worry about. Why don't you make yourself scarce around town for a few days? When you come back all the trouble with be over – bad men gone.'

Banham shook his head. Dolan cursed and went back into the shop. He was in the act of dousing the lamp when a shot crashed and a slug struck Dolan. Banham heard the smack of lead striking flesh. He turned in the direction from which the shot was fired, and dropped flat as a second shot crackled past his head. The flash of the gun gave him a marker on the gunman's position and he triggered his pistol, sending flaring stabs of brilliance slashing through the shadows.

Dolan had dropped to the ground when the shot struck him, and he remained silent and invisible in the shadows. Banham heard a gun thud on the ground, and went forward quickly. A man was down on the ground, motionless. Gun echoes faded away as Banham reached the man and kicked away a discarded gun. He heard feet running somewhere in the background, and curious voices began calling. He bent over the figure and heard a groan. There was enough light coming from a nearby lamp to enable him to recognize Abel Varney.

Varney was unconscious, a patch of blood showing darkly on his pale blue shirt. Men were beginning to appear on the street. Then Banham heard Sheriff Bain's voice and called to the lawman. Bain emerged from the shadows, gun in hand.

'What was the shooting about?' Bain demanded.

'Dolan came into town with the idea of cleaning out some bad men. He decided Varney was a bad hat, and Varney is lying in the shadows here. Dolan is down just inside the gun shop. Varney shot him.'

'You didn't do any shooting?' Bain demanded.

'No,' Banham replied. 'Tidy up around here, sheriff, and I'll get about my business. Have the doctor look at those men who are hurt, and jail them after treatment.'

Bain grumbled but moved to obey, and Banham fetched his horse and took it along to the livery barn. Afterwards he went to the law office. The Mexican deputy was on duty. He was sitting at the sheriff's desk, reading an old newspaper, and looked up at Banham with hatred in his dark eyes.

'What's biting you, Lopez?' Banham demanded.

'I've got to sit in this office watching your prisoners when I should be out on the street with the sheriff, handling the bad men,' Lopez grumbled. 'Why don't you hang around here while I do my duty?'

'Someone has to stay here, and I'm too busy,' Banham told him. 'You're elected, so do it without moaning.'

'Why have they sent you in here to interfere with the local law? We were doing all right against the bad men.'

'There were complaints about the way the law was being run around here, so I'm gonna sort out all the problems. You're a poor excuse for a deputy,

78

Lopez, and the sheriff isn't much better. I'll get around to the two of you before long, so be prepared to change your job.'

'We ain't done anything wrong,' Lopez snarled. 'Bain won't like it when I tell him what you said.'

'Where is Bain? Did he bring in Dolan and Varney?'

'They are in the cells, waiting for the doctor to get here.'

'So where is Bain?' Banham repeated.

'He's got other duties apart from doing your job for you, and he's behind time now.'

Banham picked up the bunch of keys lying on the desk. Lopez made a grab for them but was too slow. He glared at Banham.

'I need to talk to my prisoners,' Banham said. 'You stay here. I don't want you getting under my feet.'

He unlocked the door between the office and the cells. A lamp was burning on a shelf in the big room containing seven cages with barred doors. Banham paused to look around. He saw Dolan sitting on a bunk in the nearest cell, and next to the rancher was Dillman. Banham went to the door of Dolan's cell and looked in at his prisoner. Dolan was nursing his left arm, and there was blood staining his right shoulder.

'You wouldn't listen to me,' Banham said, 'and you've only got yourself to blame for the trouble you're in. You can't think much of your daughter, getting yourself put behind bars.'

'I was desperate,' Dolan replied, shaking his head. 'No one was doing anything about the bad men, so it was up to me. We could have worked together, Marshal, instead of finishing up like this.'

'I gave you the chance to do it right but you wanted it the way it's turned out, so you've got to take it as it comes. I have to do the best I can, and if local men won't help me then I have to handle the situation how I see it, and some innocent people are likely to get hurt if I get it wrong.' He glanced into the next cell. Dillman was unconscious, breathing heavily, his rugged face unnaturally pale. 'So what is it with Dillman?' he demanded. 'Where does he fit in around here?'

'I'll keep what I know to myself until I'm able to do something about the situation. I won't be in here very long.' There was an obdurate note in Dolan's voice that told Banham that the rancher was not about to cooperate.

Banham turned on his heel and departed. He locked the cell block door and went back to the desk, where Lopez was sitting motionless, intent on reading a newspaper.

The street door opened as Banham threw the cell keys on to a corner of the desk, and Sheriff Bain entered the office, accompanied by a small man whose hair was iron grey. His face was rugged and wrinkled, sharp features the colour of old mahogany. He was wearing denims and a flat-brimmed plains hat. Bain was holding his pistol in his right hand, and when he saw Banham his muzzle lifted into the aim and covered him.

'Just the man I want to see,' Bain snarled, a grin lighting up his face. His eyes were gleaming. 'Lift your hand away from your gun, Marshal, and stand very still. You make one wrong move now and you'll be marching into Hell pretty damn quick.'

Lopez got up from the desk and pulled his gun. 'What's going on?' he demanded.

'I'll tell you what's going on,' Bain said. 'I've got this no-good johnny-come-lately right where I want him. Pete knows him from somewhere in the past, and he's gonna make a statement listing everything Banham has done wrong over the past two years. Well, what are you waiting for, Lopez?' Bain motioned with his gun. 'Put Banham in a cell, and turn Dolan loose. I'm throwing in my lot with Dolan. He's made me an offer I can't turn down.'

'You're gonna take the word of this bleary eyed drunk?' Lopez was frowning. 'I don't want nothing to do with it, Sheriff, or anything Dolan's got on offer.' He lifted his left hand to his chest, removed his deputy badge, and threw it on the desk. 'I quit. I'm not getting mixed up in any more of your schemes. I'm going back to Tijuana.'

'Put that badge on again.' Bain swung his gun to cover Lopez. 'If you don't do like I say I'll put you in a cell with Banham, and you and him will disappear in the night. You'll both be dead come sun up.'

'I've done everything you've asked me since we became lawmen,' Lopez protested. 'But I've had enough. I'm getting out while the going is good.'

Bain's expression hardened. He watched Lopez move towards the street door, his levelled pistol covering the Mexican. Banham tensed, seeing an opportunity for himself as the muzzle of Bain's gun moved away. Bain squeezed his trigger, filling the office with smoke and noise. Lopez stiffened, staggered forward a couple of steps on suddenly nerveless legs, and then pitched to the floor.

Banham grasped the butt of his holstered gun and eared back the hammer as he pulled the weapon clear of his holster. The sheriff saw the sudden movement and threw himself to his left, his face showing desperation as he became aware of Banham's hostile movement. The marshal's gun crashed raucously, shaking the office, and gun smoke plumed towards the sheriff. Bain went over backwards, falling against the street door before sprawling sideways to the floor.

Gun echoes faded slowly. Banham remained motionless, gun upraised, smoke dribbling from the muzzle, and he was wondering how he could take advantage of this grim development. He didn't have long to wait to find out. The street door was thrust open and two of Dolan's men, who had come into town with the rancher, burst into the office, guns drawn and ready for action. . . .

SIX

Banham's nerves were on edge, his reflexes fluttering with anticipation, and he met the new threat with his habitual speed. Acting spontaneously, he fired and sent the nearest man to the floorboards. The second man found his target was temporarily covered by his dying companion's falling figure, and by the time he was able to fire he was too late. Banham triggered his weapon, and again the law office was racked by the grim sound of shooting. But it was over so quickly it seemed as if it had never occurred, and Banham took his time reloading his empty chambers. He was surprised, when he looked around, to find that the man Bain had brought in as a witness had taken advantage of the shooting to make himself scarce.

The office was dense with gun smoke. Banham looked around quickly, then went to the door, dragged the two dead cowboys out of the office and dumped them on the sidewalk, then went back into the office. He slammed and bolted the door. When he bent over Lopez he found the deputy was dead, and went to the sheriff's side. Bain was unconscious, breathing heavily. Blood was seeping from a neat half-inch hole that Banham's slug had punched in his upper chest.

Banham opened the street door and peered around the street. Several townsmen were standing in front of the office, talking excitedly, and they started asking questions when Banham appeared before them. He shouted for silence, and slowly the noise diminished.

'One of you, fetch the doctor. The rest of you can get the hell out of here. The shooting is over for tonight,' Banham declared.

He went back into the office and dragged the body of Lopez out to the sidewalk. One man was still standing in front of the office. Banham confronted him.

'Is there an undertaker in town?' Banham demanded.

'There sure is. Hap Miller, and he's up to his neck in business.'

'Fetch him here pronto.' Banham went back into the office. He picked up the cell keys and went back into the cell block. Dolan was standing at the door of his cell, looking anxious.

'Where's Bain,' Dolan asked.

'He's on the floor of the outer office. He told me he was doing a deal with you. So give me the details. You're in a lot of trouble now, Dolan, and the best way out of it is to tell me what's going on. If you've got any feelings at all for your daughter you'll open up and fill me in on what's going on so I can handle it.'

Dolan turned away from the cell door and dropped heavily on the bunk in the cell. Banham heard a noise in the outer office, pulled his gun, and went to investigate. Doctor Palmer was closing the street door. He was carrying a brown leather medical bag.

'What's going on in town tonight?' Palmer asked. 'I've had several calls so far, and it sure looks like you've been busy – dead men on the sidewalk outside the office, and the jail half-filled with work waiting for me.'

Palmer didn't wait for an answer but dropped to one knee beside the prostrate sheriff. Banham sat on a corner of the desk and watched. Palmer carried out a swift examination of Bain and then got to his feet.

'I'll have the sheriff taken over to my office,' he said.

'There are a couple of men in the cells who need checking, Doc. One of them, Dillman, looks to be in a bad way. I need to question him so check him out next and make him comfortable.'

Palmer hastened into the cells, and Banham unlocked Dillman's cell. A voice called from outside the office and Banham went back to answer. He opened the street door to a man dressed in a grey suit, who stared at Banham before speaking.

'Where's Sheriff Bain?' he demanded.

Banham opened the door wider so the man could look into the office. The man gasped and put a hand on the doorpost as shock hit him.

'Is the sheriff dead?' he demanded. 'Who shot him?'

'I did. Bain is not dead yet. Who are you?'

'Henry Parfitt. I own the hotel, and I'm also the town mayor. So who are you?'

'Marshal Banham. I'm here to restore law and order.'

'Where's that Mexican deputy?'

'He's out on the sidewalk, dead.'

'Did you kill him?'

'No. Bain did.'

'What's going on around here? Why did you shoot Bain?'

'He was gonna shoot me. Save your questions now. I'll want to talk to you when I've got more time. Tomorrow morning.'

'I wanted to ask Bain about a matter I put to him several days ago,' Parfitt said.

'Bain is no longer the sheriff. If he survives his wound he'll be in jail facing a charge of killing his deputy and, no doubt, when I start investigating him, I expect other charges will arise. What was it you asked Bain? Maybe I can help you.'

'My wife has a brother who's visiting with us. Frank Fullerton. He was a town marshal in Kansas, worked with Bat Masterson and Wyatt Earp at one time. He fancies coming back to Texas to work for the law, and I promised to see if I can get him fixed up here.'

'I know of him,' Banham said. 'Tell him to come and see me as soon as he can. With Bain out of the picture we can do with an experienced man to take over.'

'I'll send him here as soon as I see him. He's keen to start working.' Parfitt departed quickly.

Palmer emerged from the cell block, medical bag in his hand.

'Dillman is seriously hurt. I'll have to get him over to my place if I'm going to have any chance of saving him.'

'Sure, Doc, anything you say.' Banham opened the door and Palmer departed, pausing in the doorway to add, 'I'll fetch some men to convey Dillman and Bain to my office.'

'I'll be here until you come for them.' Banham went back into the cells and confronted Dolan, who was stretched out on his back, his eyes closed.

'It's time for you to start talking, Dolan,' Banham rapped, and the rancher opened his eyes and stared up at Banham's harsh face. 'If you don't give out on what you know I'll make life hard for you. The charges I've got lined up for you will keep you behind bars for twenty years, unless they hang you for what you've done. Several men have been killed this evening, and some of their deaths can be laid at your door.'

'Where is Bain? He ain't dead, is he?'

'Unless Doc Palmer does a lot of work on him he won't see another sun up. He told me he had made a deal with you, and I want to know what it's about. This is your last chance to come clean about what you've been mixed up in.'

'You're talking to the wrong man,' Dolan said sharply. 'Dillman is the one you want. I already told you that. How come you're pushing me instead of the guilty man?'

'I've got to start somewhere, and you're the only one who is able to talk right now. I will get at the truth eventually, and if you don't help me now you'll be sorry for the rest of your life.'

'I'll talk to you in the morning.' Dolan passed a hand across his eyes. 'I ain't feeling too good right now. I need to sleep.'

'Your time is running out,' Banham said. He cursed under his breath when he heard knocking at the street door and turned quickly to go and answer.

The doctor was waiting with two men and a stretcher. They collected Dillman and took him out. As they moved out of the office a woman's voice spoke from the shadows on the sidewalk, and Banham looked up to see his sister, Hannah, appearing out of the gloom.

'Hannah, what are you doing here?' he demanded.

'I heard shooting going on and feared you had been killed. I expect you were in the thick of it. What happened?'

'It was mainly the sheriff and his deputy resigning their jobs. Lopez won't be strumming his guitar out

88

at the ranch any more. He's dead.'

'Did you kill him?' Hannah's voice was thick with tension.

'I didn't, as it happens. Sheriff Bain shot him. How is Aggie?'

'She's sleeping now. She was worried about you when we heard the shooting, and she wanted to get her rifle and come and help you, but she shouldn't get out of her bed. I came to check on you so I can put her mind at rest when she wakes.'

'You did wrong to leave the store,' he reproved. 'Aggie wouldn't have been shot if she'd listened to me. The men I'm up against are real desperadoes, and they wouldn't hesitate to grab anyone they could use to put pressure on me. Come into the office and wait for me and I'll take you back to the store. The doctor is coming back shortly, and then I'll have time for you.'

Hannah entered the office, grimacing at the acrid smell of the recent shooting. She sat down at the desk and Banham waited impatiently for the doctor to return.

The street door opened and a big man stepped into the doorway. He was wearing a dark suit, a flat-brimmed hat, and had a gun-belt strapped around his lean waist. He was in his thirties, with dark eyes and black hair. He looked as if he could handle himself in any situation. He was at least three inches over six feet in height, solid-looking, and apparently ready for anything.

'Howdy?' he said. 'I'm Frank Fullerton. My

brother-in-law is Frank Parfitt, the town mayor.'

'The mayor mentioned you when he dropped by. You're looking for a job with the local law, huh?'

'Sure. I've done most of my law work in Kansas, and I feel it's time for a change.'

'Your arrival here is timely. The town lost its sheriff and deputy this evening. I've heard of you, Frank. You've made quite a name for yourself in Kansas. I'm Dale Banham, a deputy US Marshal sent in here to handle local problems, and I've sure got my hands full. If you're available you can start work immediately. I've got a feeling you'll suit me.'

'I've got some newspaper clippings from Kansas that cover some of my exploits.' Fullerton placed a large envelope on the desk. 'If you've got a law badge I'll pin it on and get to work immediately.'

'That's fine.' Banham turned to Hannah. 'This is my sister, Hannah. She's staying with her friend at the general store. Perhaps you'll see that she gets back there safely and save me the chore. Then come back here. We'll have a chat about the situation, and I'll swear you in.'

Hannah grimaced but made no protest, and Fullerton escorted her out of the office.

Banham dropped into the seat behind the desk and heaved a sigh. He was getting nowhere fast and his patience was ebbing. He gazed at the pool of blood on the floor where Bain's wound had leaked. He needed information, but it was hard to come by. He sat motionless, tired beyond comprehension, until Fullerton returned from escorting Hannah back to the general store, and then stirred himself. Here was some real help at last.

'You've come into this at a tough moment, Frank,' Banham said ruefully. 'I arrived only a couple of days ago, and the sheriff and his deputy were up to no good on their own account, although that came to a head unexpectedly and the picture is beginning to clear.'

'I haven't been back in Texas more than a couple of weeks so I don't have much of an idea what's happening around here.' There was a steel-like gleam in Fullerton's eyes. 'I have noticed some things in town that smack of trouble for the law. It's kind of second nature to watch points when you've been a lawman.'

'I know what you mean.' Banham jerked open the desk drawer and looked over a miscellaneous collection of law badges inside. He picked up one that bore the legend Town Marshal and tossed it to Fullerton. 'Hold up your right hand and I'll swear you in. Then you can start law dealing.'

'That suits me fine. I'll take a look around town. It's the town marshal's job to make a round of the businesses to check for trouble. I'll stay on duty until sun up, then get a couple of hours sleep, and after that I'll be ready for anything. Is there a night jailer to take over in here?'

'I don't know yet. We could certainly do with some extra help. I'll talk to Frank Parfitt in the morning and get things moving.' Banham got to his feet. 'Raise your right hand and repeat after me.'

Fullerton smiled as he repeated the familiar oath that Banham uttered, and then pinned the law star to his shirt front.

'I'll get busy now,' he said.

Banham found a large key in the desk drawer and gave it to Fullerton.

'Try that in the lock. You'll need a key.'

Fullerton tested the key, which worked, and then departed to begin his duties.

Banham gave Fullerton a few moments before leaving the office and, pausing to lock the street door, he could see the new lawman's big figure along the sidewalk, and followed discreetly. It wasn't that he didn't trust Fullerton – he was worried that the bad men would get to him before he could find his stride with the new job. He could hear Fullerton trying doors of shops and businesses. There were few townsfolk on the street. The amount of shooting that had taken place recently had persuaded all but the foolhardy to stay at home.

Banham was half-expecting trouble to break out so he was not surprised when a pistol boomed and flashed up ahead, just about where Fullerton was checking the door of the butcher shop. Another shot hammered close on the heels of the first, and then a spate of shooting flared. Banham drew his gun and went forward at a run, eyes narrowed against brilliant gun flashes.

A pistol was firing from very close to the ground – Fullerton's position, and three other weapons were in action, shooting from across the street – an opposite alley. Banham thought the shooting had been intended for him. He dropped to one knee, only twenty yards from Fullerton, and when a gap in the gun racket occurred he called out his identity to the new lawman.

'Come and join me, Marshal,' Fullerton replied. 'I've got both hands full in this game, but it seems the opposition is pulling out. I've nailed the man who started the shooting.'

Banham went to where Fullerton was getting to his feet in the shadows. The shooting had died away and an uneasy silence settled over the street.

'A second man took off along the street, and I caught a glimpse of him shinning over the wall around the undertaker's yard. I suggest we mosey along there and grab him.'

'I was about to suggest that.' Banham moved out of the shadows. 'I need a prisoner badly, someone who can tell me what the hell is going in around here.'

'We'll get him,' Fullerton said confidently.

They moved cautiously along the street, sticking to the shadows, until they reached the double gates shutting off the undertaker's property.

'He went over this gate like a bat out of hell.' Fullerton stretched to his full height and peered over the gates. He could see over without tiptoeing. A gun blasted instantly, and Fullerton dropped to his knees. 'I'll climb over the wall to our right and flush him out,' he said. 'It's a one-man job, so perhaps you'll stay out here and catch him when he breaks cover.'

'I should be the one to go in after him,' Banham protested.

'I've got to show you how I operate,' Fullerton replied.

'It's all yours,' Banham responded.

Fullerton moved to the right along the wall and then climbed over it, dropping out of sight on the other side. Banham waited eagerly, gun ready. He could hear nothing. Then two shots rang out with startling suddenness. He lifted his pistol, his hands suddenly clammy. The next instant a figure came vaulting over the wall, almost dropping on the spot where he was standing.

It was not Fullerton, Banham could see at a glance. The man lost his balance when he landed, startled by Banham's presence, and he sprawled heavily when he fell over Banham's suddenly out-thrust foot. He rolled and came to his feet, reaching for his holstered gun, and as the muzzle swung to cover Banham the marshal triggered his pistol, aiming for the man's legs. There was an agonized cry and the man began writhing on the ground. Banham kicked the man's gun hand and his weapon flew wide. Banham leaned forward, reversed his gun, and struck the man's head.

A moment later Fullerton came over the wall, his gun in his right hand, and he halted quickly, his teeth gleaming in a smile.

'That wasn't too bad,' Fullerton observed.

'Let's get him to the law office and talk to him,'

Banham replied.

The man was dazed from the blow he had received, and Fullerton half-carried, half-dragged him along the sidewalk. He soon recovered his wits when he was seated in the chair before the desk in the office and was confronted by the two lawmen. He was range-dressed, his face was wrinkled, but he was not old, no more than thirty. There was a smear of blood on his forehead where Banham had struck him. His hair was black and unkempt.

'What's your name and why were you shooting at our new town marshal?' Banham demanded.

'I wasn't shooting at anyone. I'm Larry Hogan, and I was on my way to visit Hannah Banham at the general store when shooting broke out right under my nose. Two or three men began shooting at a figure across the street from me and I was in their line of fire, caught up in the middle of it. I hit the ground, crawled clear, and high-tailed it out of there. But someone chased me and I went into the undertaker's yard. I guess you know what happened after that.'

'Larry Hogan,' Banham repeated. 'Hannah is my sister. She mentioned a Larry Hogan as being her neighbour.'

'I recognize you now,' Hogan said. 'I didn't expect to be on the wrong end of your gun. I felt a bullet burn on my right leg when you fired at me after I came back over the wall. I almost took a slug through the head when the shooting started.'

'That's what life is like around here these days,'

Fullerton observed. 'It's a sad comment on the local law office, but things will be different from now on. Let's take a look at your leg.'

Hogan produced a knife from a sheath on his belt and bent over his right leg. He slit open the lower area of his pants and revealed a red mark across the side of his calf where small beads of blood were seeping out of a slight wound.

'You were lucky, and then some,' Fullerton observed.

'It didn't seem like that at the time,' Hogan said. 'I've heard all about the trouble in this county, but I never expected to get caught up in it.'

'If you're going to see Hannah then I'll walk with you to the door of the general store,' Banham said.

'I'll continue my round,' Fullerton said. 'See you back at the law office, Marshal.'

Banham walked with Hogan along the street to the general store. Hogan was limping slightly.

'Can you tell me anything about what's been going on around here lately?' Banham asked.

'I've heard talk, naturally, but I don't get into town very often, and it's quite lonely out on the range. I haven't seen any trouble out there. All I do know is that Hannah has been getting trouble from Dolan of the Big D ranch, so she told me. I said I'd go and talk to him, but she was against the idea – said I'd only stir up trouble. But it's my experience that if the small rancher gives way to pressure from the big ranchers it only adds to the problem.'

'I've sorted that particular problem,' Banham

said. 'I think it came from whatever the local law men were doing, and I haven't got around to checking on that. I'll be attending to smaller problems shortly, and when I get to get them. I expect to learn the truth.'

They found the front of the store locked, and a dim light was showing in the back place.

'We'll go around the back,' Banham suggested.

'I'd rather not disturb Hannah now,' Hogan said quickly. 'I'll fetch my horse and head on back to my spread. I'll come back in a couple of days.'

'Is your horse in the livery barn?'

'Yeah. It's not good sense to leave it on the street like in the old days.'

'I'll walk with you to the barn and then circle around that end of town to meet up with Fullerton,' Banham said.

'I knew Fullerton in Kansas. He's a good man – got a fine reputation up that way, but Bain and Lopez were up to no good. I reckon they had their fingers in the pie around here.'

'I gained that impression when I first set eyes on them,' Banham admitted. 'I shall talk to Bain in a few days to clear up a couple of points with him.'

They walked along the sidewalk toward the livery barn. Banham was alert, his eyes unceasing as he watched their surroundings, ears strained for the slightest unnatural sound, and his right hand was close to the butt of his holstered gun, ready for anything. He could hear the muted sound of a piano being thumped in the big saloon, and an anonymous figure emerged from between the batwings, crossed the sidewalk and swung into the saddle of a waiting horse. The clatter of hoofs echoed across the street and faded quickly as the rider rode out of town.

Banham was distracted by the rider. He was passing an alley, and realized he was no longer alone. Figures came silently out of the shadows to surround him and Hogan. He reached for his pistol, but despite his great speed he could not get into action quickly enough. One of his assailants swung a rifle and the butt slammed against his head. The shadows seemed to explode into a series of brilliant flashing lights, and then a black cloud swept over him and he fell on his face. He was not aware of his gun slipping harmlessly from his hand. . . .

SEVEN

Banham awoke to the sound of a low buzzing noise in his ears. His eyes flickered open and he looked around uncomprehendingly, his presence of mind strangely absent. He tried to recall what had happened but his brain remained maddeningly unfocused, and the surrounding darkness added to his bewilderment. He tried vainly to move but his hands could not obey his thoughts, and he realized with shock chasing through his veins that he was hog-tied, awareness dragging him out of his inertia and releasing his mental ability to its former efficiency. Then he realized that he was face down on a horse and being led out of town, the jolting movement filling him with nausea.

His memory returned and he recalled the incident that had led to his present discomfiture. Where was Hogan? He tried to lift his head to check his surroundings but dizziness assailed him and he slumped, the darkness of unconsciousness stealing

99

his awareness. Sight and sound vanished again, and the sun was shining when next he awakened.

A noise like a series of massive hammer blows, like a sledgehammer beating a tin roof, filled his returning senses, and some minutes passed before he realized it was caused by the throbbing in his head. His left eyelid was glued down with dried blood, and he tried tentatively to check his surroundings. He was assailed by dizziness, and relaxed and closed his eyes. Trying to think about the situation proved to be beyond his efforts and he relaxed and let the weakness that was trying to overpower him have its way. He lay as dead, his brain ticking over, until a loud noise jerked him out of his lethargy and he made an effort to regain control of his body.

He opened his eyes cautiously, and was relieved to discover that the dizziness had receded. He gazed around at an unfamiliar room that was furnished as a bedroom, and he was lying on a bed, his wrists bound in front of him. Sunlight blazed in through a window to dazzle him, and the glare set his head throbbing again. As he closed his eyes he saw the door of the room was open, and a figure, a man holding a pistol, was standing in the doorway.

Banham opened his eyes again quickly. He had got a glimpse of the man and recognized Larry Hogan, He stared at Hogan, who came to the foot of the bed, his expression grim, his levelled gun steady in his right hand.

'You're giving me a lot of trouble, Marshal,' said

Hogan, shaking his head. 'I thought I'd finish what I started around here before the State law could show up, but you've beaten me to the draw, and I'm gonna have to get rid of you before you can do any more damage to my plans.'

'So you're an outlaw,' Banham said. 'I had a feeling there was a real bad man somewhere in the background in this business, and you've jumped out of the woodpile.'

'You forced me to confront you. I never saw a lawman clean up so fast or so good as you. You're like a one-man army. Hannah told me you were brilliant, but she underestimated you. I thought I could handle you with no trouble at all, but I've had to pull out all the stops. You're like a runaway train, and I've got to derail you before you finish me.'

'Where am I?' Banham asked.

'At my ranch, down the trail from your spread. But you'll be dead and buried before sundown. I've got to stop the rot in my gang so there's no other way I can handle you.'

'What's your real name?'

Hogan smiled. 'You don't need to know. You'll go into your grave without learning who's put you there.'

'You'll be making a bad mistake if you kill me. When I die the law will send as many men as it takes to get you. They won't leave a stone unturned to nail every last one of your bunch. You don't know it, but your days are numbered. If you've got any sense at all you'll turn me loose and head for other parts.

You're all washed up around here.'

'Nice try, but I don't scare easy. My gang is out on a job right now, but when a couple of them show up they will take you to a lonely spot and bury you.'

'Where is your gang?'

'Nice try, but don't ask. I'm two jumps ahead of you. Nothing concerns you now. Make the most of your remaining hours. You don't have long.'

Hogan departed, and Banham lay motionless until the door was closed. He heard the sound of a key being turned and then boots pounded down a flight of stairs. As soon as silence returned, he pushed himself into a sitting position and examined the rope around his wrists.

He struggled to loosen the knots in the rope but could make no impression on the stiff Manila fibre. He swung his feet to the floor and stood up, looking around for some means of attacking the knot. A short rope was stretched between the walls in a corner, and it was attached to two protruding nails. A shirt was suspended from the rope. Banham went closer and examined one of the nails. Thankful that his hands were bound in front of him, he untied the rope from the nail and manipulated the knot against it until the end of the nail was forced inside the knot. He put pressure on the knot, bending his knees to add weight to the force he could apply. Sweat beaded his forehead and he closed his eyes. But nothing happened. The knot was unassailable, and the nail bent under the force he exerted on it.

He gave up the attempt and dropped wearily on

the bed. His head was aching intolerably and he was sweating. He felt as if the last ounce of his strength had drained out of his pores. Then his determination kicked in and he stood up and crossed to the window; looked out over the back yard and saw a barn. He tested the window and it opened. He slid over the sill and pushed his legs out until his point of balance swung outwards. He was some twelve feet above the ground and there was grass directly below him. He twisted to his right, swung his hands in the same direction, and then launched himself off the sill. He got a grip on the window ledge with his left hand and caught hold with his right hand as his body pulled clear.

He stopped sharply when his arms were at full stretch, released his grip on the sill immediately, and dropped to the ground. He landed on his feet and fell on to his back. He sprang up and started running to the barn, but turned aside to a nearby haystack when his keen eyes saw a hay-cutter on the stack, a two-foot blade with a long handle used for cutting the haystack into a convenient pieces. It was leaning against the stack. He dropped to his knees beside it, and it was the work of a few moments to rub his bonds against the sharp blade and release himself.

He went on to the barn and entered. The first thing he saw was a Winchester rifle hanging from a bracket just inside the door. He checked it and was pleased to see it was fully loaded. He went out back and saw his horse in a corral, still saddled and ready to travel. He turned and went back to the house, taking a route that kept him unseen until he was only ten yards from the porch. He angled to his right, made his way around to the rear of the house, and went to the back door.

The unlocked back door took him into the kitchen, and he moved silently through the lower rooms until he entered the big living room overlooking the porch. Larry Hogan was seated at a table with a plate of food before him.

'You don't have the time to finish that,' Banham rasped, moving in from behind.

Hogan came out of his chair like a grizzly bear being attacked by hornets. He swung to face Banham, his right hand dropping to his holstered pistol. When he saw Banham's grim figure, and the levelled rifle, he hurled himself sideways and crashed to the floor, finishing his draw on his back. Banham squeezed his trigger, aiming for Hogan's right hand, and the outlaw's pistol flew from his fingers. Hogan dived under the table and then stood up, grabbing the edge of the table and overturning it in Banham's direction. Banham jumped clear, but the table caught him a glancing blow on his left elbow and he lost the rifle at the impact and was thrown to the right. He fell and rolled before starting to his feet, but before he could locate Hogan the man crashed against him.

A hard fist sledged against Banham's chin, upsetting his still-throbbing head, and all he could do was reach out to grasp Hogan as he went down. His clutching left hand grasped the slack of Hogan's shirt and he hung on desperately, intent on remaining at close quarters. They hit the floor and Hogan squirmed like a puma, punching desperately with both hands. Banham recoiled. He had never been hit so hard in his life. Solid knuckles smashed into his stomach and he twisted away. A second blow took him on the chin and his senses swirled. He shook his head against the effect and grabbed a tighter hold on Hogan, throwing a punch with his right hand, knuckles clenched, and caught Hogan on the jaw.

Hogan slumped momentarily, and Banham, feeling his strength seeping out of his body like water running out of a tap, took Hogan in a bear hug and exerted his failing strength, his hands locked together in the small of Hogan's back and his Stetson jammed against the outlaw's face. Hogan struggled to break free. Banham's feet were thrusting against the floor and the whole of his body was rigid in what he knew was his last effort. They strained, one against the other, and Banham was beginning to sense that this was one fight he could not win when Hogan suddenly relaxed and slumped.

They fell apart, and Banham struggled to his feet, looking around desperately for the rifle he had dropped. He saw Hogan's pistol a few feet away and snatched it up, turning to face the outlaw, shoulders heaving from the effect of his efforts to overcome his adversary. Hogan was semi-conscious, and Banham sat down on a nearby chair to recoup his strength, eyes closed and head throbbing.

Minutes passed. Hogan began to stir. Banham heaved a sigh. He covered Hogan with the pistol and waited for the man to open his eyes. When Hogan started to his feet a harsh voice halted him and he turned his head to see Banham seated only feet away, a pistol aimed at him. For a moment he remained motionless, his body rigid, and then he heaved a long sigh and collapsed on the floor.

'I'll shoot you if you don't stay still,' Banham warned. 'You're under arrest and I'm gonna take you back to town.'

'You'll never hold me,' Hogan retorted.

'We'll see,' Banham replied.

He got to his feet, relieved that his strength was returning, and at that moment his keen ears picked up the sound of horses entering the yard. He moved to the window and peered out. Two riders were approaching. Banham picked up the Winchester he had dropped and holstered the pistol.

'Stay where you are, Hogan,' he said. 'Two men are coming to the house, and I want to get the drop on them. If you try anything when they get here I'll shoot you dead. Make no mistake about that.'

He could hear the voices of the men as they approached the house, the clop of hoofs as they crossed the yard, and when they reined up in front of the porch he opened the door and motioned for Hogan to get up and precede him to confront the newcomers.

Hogan staggered through the doorway, and then threw himself flat on the porch, yelling as he did so. 'I'm in trouble here. Start shooting.'

Banham was in view of the outlaws as Hogan called, and saw both men reach for their guns. He triggered the rifle, roughly aligning the long barrel as he fired. The nearest man collected the first .40-40 slug and went out of his saddle, falling against the rider beside him, spoiling his aim as he was bringing his pistol to bear on Banham, who fired again. The second man slid out of his saddle with blood spurting from his forehead. Banham turned his attention to Hogan, who was on his hands and knees and in the act of lunging towards the nearest horse, reaching up to snatch a rifle out of the saddle boot.

Hogan turned with the rifle in his hand. Banham threw himself sideways, dropped to one knee, and triggered a shot that struck Hogan in the chest. The crooked rancher went over backwards, dropping the rifle. He fell heavily and did not move again.

Banham went forward to check the two fallen riders. His eyes narrowed as he discovered they were dead. He bent over Hogan, and heaved a sigh, for the rancher was also dead. He had used up all his chances. There were a number of questions in Banham's mind that he wished he could have put to the outlaw.

He fetched his horse from the corral, left the grim scene he had wrought in his defence of the law, and rode out in the direction of town. When he saw Hannah's ranch to his left he turned aside to check it in passing, and a man stepped out of the house, gun in hand, when Banham reined in at the porch.

'Who are you?' the man demanded, covering Banham with his drawn pistol.

'I'm Dale Banham, a deputy marshal. Hannah Banham is my sister, and she owns this place. What are you doing here?'

'My name is Pete Skinner. Larry Hogan sent me here to keep an eye on the spread while Hannah is in town.'

Skinner, tall and lean, with a lined face and dark eyes, holstered his gun and relaxed, but he blinked in shock when Banham palmed his pistol with a slick movement.

'Hogan is dead and you're under arrest,' Banham said. 'Get rid of your gun now, and do it slow, finger and thumb only.'

'The boss is dead?' Skinner shook his head in disbelief. 'What happened to him?'

'Just do as you're told and we'll head for town.'

Skinner disarmed himself. His gun thudded on the porch.

'Step away from it,' Banham ordered, and moved forward to kick the weapon into the yard. His movement brought him into the open doorway of the house, and he froze when a hand holding a pistol was thrust through the doorway and the gun muzzle pressed against his left temple.

'Drop your gun and then don't move a muscle,'

108

said a strident voice in his ear. 'Did you kill Hogan?'

'I'm a deputy marshal, sent in here to clean up on the bad men. If you've got any sense you'll put down your guns.' Banham threw his pistol down on the porch. 'Your boss is dead and you're out of a job. I'll take you into town and check you out. If you're not outlaws you'll save yourselves a lot of trouble. You might even be allowed to shake the dust of this range off your boots. But if you kill me you'll be hunted down and hanged. It's not a good choice, but it's the only one you've got.'

'I ain't surrendering to the law,' Skinner said. 'Get some rope and hot-tie him, Steve. Then we'll light out for other parts. Anyone can see the game is over around here. Let's get moving.'

The man covering Banham emerged from the house. He was a small individual, range dressed and dirty, with a straggly beard and lank hair under a weather-stained Stetson.

'I ain't gonna lay a hand on him if he's a lawman,' Steve said. 'Take his guns and then we'll hightail it. Let's mosey.'

Skinner agreed readily. Banham stood motionless while they took his weapons, and they escorted him at gunpoint through the house and out back to the corral where their mounts were waiting. Skinner took a thin strip of leather from his saddlebag and tied Banham's wrists together, then fastened the loose end of the strip to the corral.

'It won't hold you for long,' Skinner said, 'but it'll give us time to get clear. We're leaving the county.'

'Before you go just tell me who's behind the trouble around here. If you do I'll forget all about you two, and you'll get away with answering for what you've done, and bear in mind that murder will figure in the charges I'll be slapping on the men I do arrest.'

Skinner shook his head. 'No talk,' he said. 'One word from either of us and we'll have the hard cases looking for us. You'll have to do your own dirty work, Marshal. Just be thankful we're pulling out and leaving you alive.'

Banham watched them mount and ride out. He turned his attention to his bonds and was relieved to find them loosely tied. He used his teeth to undo the knots and hurried to his horse. Mounting, he did not even consider chasing Skinner and his sidekick but set out to complete his trip to town. He had a sudden urge to confront Dolan, and this time he would compel the rancher to do some talking. . . .

EIGHT

The sun was almost overhead, mercilessly baking Main Street, when Banham rode into Clear Water Creek. He stopped off at the doc's house because his left eye was partially glued with dried blood and his head was aching relentlessly. He would have liked nothing better than to hit the sack and relax until his aches and pains eased, but he knew from bitter experience that law duty was an indomitable, unforgiving mistress, and he could not relax until he had mastered the situation that existed on this range.

Doc Palmer was finishing his noon meal when Banham disturbed him.

'You look like you found trouble on the range,' Palmer observed.

'Nothing I couldn't handle, Doc. I took a helluva whack on the head last night and was out like a light until sun up.'

'Come into my office and I'll take a look at you.' Palmer led the way through the lower part of the house. 'Have you talked to anyone since you rode in?'

'No. I need something for my head. It hurts real bad.'

'You've got a touch of concussion,' Palmer said after examining him. 'You'll have to take it easy for a few days. I'll give you something for your head, and you'd better rest up until you feel better. I doubt you'll take my advice, because when you learn what's happened in town during the night you'll jump on your horse and try to ride in all directions at once.'

'What the hell happened?' Banham started to get up but Palmer pushed him back in the seat and held him there.

'Relax, Marshal. Just sit still and listen to me. Your new deputy was gunned down some time after midnight. I've got him in my hospital. He's clinging to life with a bullet wound in his chest, too close to his heart for comfort. But I think he'll survive. He's young, strong, and very fit. I've also got one of the men who attacked him. Fullerton shot him and I've got him sedated. He's a townsman named Frank Harvey, and I don't think he'll survive twenty-four hours.'

'I'd like to talk to him.' Banham thrust off the doctor's restraining hand and staggered to his feet.

'You can't. He's unconscious, and not likely to regain his senses in this world.'

'What does he do around town?' Banham demanded.

112

'He's a respectable townsman, married with two children, and he runs a freighting business. I can't imagine what he was doing, involved in shooting a lawman.'

'I'll find out,' said Banham grimly. 'This is the first break I've had in this business, Let me know if Harvey shows any sign of coming back to his senses, Doc.'

'You'll be the first to know,' Palmer said gravely. 'But take it easy or before you know it you'll be lying in one of my hospital beds.'

Banham nodded and departed. He hurried across the street to the law office, entered, and found Henry Parfitt, the town mayor-cum-hotel owner, sitting behind the desk.

'It's about time you showed up, Marshal,' Parfitt growled. 'Hell broke out in here last night. My wife's brother is at the doctor's place, near to death's door, and you've been out of town.'

'Doing my job,' Banham snapped. 'Why are you here?'

'Someone has got to run the law, and there's no one else.'

'Can't you get hold of a couple of good, law-abiding townsmen to stand in? There must be some men around here that you can trust.'

Parfitt shook his head. 'No one will take any chances when a man like Fullerton is shot in cold blood. He's a tough, experienced lawman.'

'You can leave now. I'll take over. In the morning, try and get someone to help me.'

Parfitt got to his feet and departed without speaking. Banham followed him outside.

'Get the liveryman to collect my horse, will you?'

Parfitt nodded and went off along the sidewalk. Banham closed the street door and locked it. He picked up the cell keys from the desk and went through to the cells. Dolan was asleep on the bunk in his cell. Banham rattled the cell keys on the bars, and Dolan jerked awake. He glared balefully at Banham, but he was looking worried, Banham noted, and that was a good sign.

'Where have you been?' Dolan demanded. 'Raising more hell, huh?'

'That's all my life consists of,' Banham retorted, 'and mainly because of men like you. I've lost count of the bad men I've killed. Each day I try to even the differences between the law-abiding and the outlaws. It's as never-ending war, and there's no end in sight—'

'Spare me the sob story,' Dolan snarled. 'I've got my own problems. When are you gonna turn me loose? I was after the bad men, those hard cases you don't seem to be able to get.'

'If I got support from local men my job would be much easier. Are your problems to do with your daughter? You told me she was in Austin.'

'I got a wire from Austin. It was delivered from the telegraph office. That's why I came into town with a few men. Julie was visited by a man who told her he was from me, and that I'd been shot and was dying. She believed the man and left with him, apparently to come here. The man who took her is obviously one of Dillman's outlaws, and she could be in bad trouble right now.'

'You knew that earlier?' Banham demanded. 'Why in hell didn't you tell me?'

'I fight my own troubles. Turn me loose and I'll get after my daughter.'

'No dice! You're staying put until you level with me. I need information on the local set-up, and you're the man to give it me. When I arrived you were the first man I pegged as the big boss of the outlaws. OK, so apparently you're not. But I still think you're mixed up in this somewhere. You had Dillman working for you.'

'I told you about him. He has a gang with him and they are using my daughter as a lever against me.'

'Why?'

A shadow crossed Dolan's face and he shook his head. 'I ain't about to tell you that.'

'You're worried about your daughter but you ain't above risking her life to keep your dirty secrets, huh?'

'I don't know which way to turn,' Dolan admitted.

'You know Larry Hogan, huh?'

'Sure I do. He's seeing your sister Hannah.'

'I killed him earlier. He was running a gang around here.'

Dolan stared at him, shocked speechless by the news. Then he gulped and gasped. 'Heck, I always had my doubts about Hogan. So he's one of the rats chasing after the rainbow.'

'I'm wondering how many gangs are working around here. And what's the attraction?' Banham persisted. 'Don't tell me you don't know because my instincts tell me you're caught up in this trouble, and I'll get at the truth before it's over. You could save yourself a lot of trouble by trusting me with what you know, and you've got to do something about your daughter. It's obvious to me that you're between a rock and a hard place.'

'Turn me loose and I'll soon get rid of the troublemakers.' Dolan clenched his hands as he gazed into Banham's eyes.

Banham shook his head. 'If things go wrong with your daughter, don't forget I offered to help you. It's not too late for you to change your mind. But you're bull-headed, and it's your girl's life you're playing with.' He paused and his eyes narrowed as a thought struck him. 'Nothing should be more precious in your life than the safety and welfare of your daughter. It's not natural to put anything above her, but that's what you're doing. So what is there around here you value above the girl?'

Dolan's face changed and his eyes narrowed as he shook his head. 'You're loco if you think that. I'd lay down my life to protect Julie. But my hands are tied because my enemies have backed me into a corner. I need to be free so I can strike at them, and if anything bad happens to my girl I'll remember that you wouldn't stretch your rules an inch to help me.'

Banham heaved a sigh and turned away, aware that he was wasting his time, but he paused and studied Dolan's tense face for a moment. Sweat was beading the rancher's forehead, and there was pain in his eyes.

'How long have you been running cattle on this range?' Banham demanded.

Dolan gazed at him, his eyes suddenly expressionless. 'What's that got to do with anything?'

'Just answer the question. If you don't start changing your attitude I'll dig into your past, and believe me, if I get something on you I'll hit you with every charge of criminal activity I can lay my hands on, and then some.'

'I've led a blameless life. Go ahead and check all you like. You won't pin anything on me.'

Banham's patience became exhausted and he returned to the front office. He needed to tell Hannah about Larry Hogan, and perhaps his sister could tell him something about Dolan's past. He left the office, locked the door, and walked along the street to the general store. Hannah was behind the long counter, helping to serve the several waiting customers, and she came to him immediately.

'I need to talk with you, Hannah,' he said.

'You sound quite serious,' she responded. 'What's wrong?'

He led her along the store until they were out of earshot of the customers. Hannah looked at him closely, as if anticipating bad news. He put a hand to her shoulder and squeezed gently. She frowned and seemed to cringe away from him.

'What's happened?' she asked. 'Tell me. Don't keep me in suspense.'

He pointed to a row of seats around a big pot-bellied stove provided for the convenience of customers. 'Let's sit there,' he suggested.

She sat on the nearest chair and he sat beside her. He caught hold of one of her hands as he told her about Larry Hogan. She remained silent, but he saw shock creep into her eyes, and disbelief and pain. He spoke harshly, unemotionally, and when he fell silent she put her hands to her face and began to weep quietly. He remained motionless, a hand on her shoulder, his sympathy brimming, nonplussed by her grief and helpless to assuage her pain.

Her weeping stopped eventually and she looked at him. Her eyes were shimmering with tears as yet unshed but she made an effort to regain her poise.

'It's such a shock,' she whispered. 'We were planning to wed next year. He was filled with plans for the future, and now he's dead, and it seems he wasn't at all like the man he appeared to be.'

'We don't know why he was on this range. I will find out but it will take time. Can I talk to you about other things, Hannah? I'm practically a stranger around here and I need help to get to grips with my investigation. If I can learn some background information on what's been going on I'll have a better chance to do what I came here for.'

'How can I help?' A sigh escaped her and she

shuddered convulsively.

'I've got Dolan in jail. I think he's implicated in the trouble around here, but he won't tell me anything. I need to find out what I can about his past. You were having trouble with him when I spoke to you at our place. What was that all about?'

'He didn't give me any trouble directly. I thought he was trying to make me sell out to him and move someplace else, but he never pushed it. I think some of his crew were trying something against me at one time, but I spoke to Sheriff Bain about it and he must have done or said something to someone because the pressure eased. Was Sheriff Bain crooked?'

'I've got to check out his recent activities, but he was intent on killing me, and he shot his deputy, so there was a lot wrong with his law dealing. What can you tell me about Dolan? He told me his foreman, Dillman, was using his daughter Julie as a lever to put pressure on him.'

'Julie Dolan is in Austin, as far as I know, getting an education,' Hannah said. 'She's been away a couple of years.'

'Dolan says he received a wire from her. A man went to Austin and told her Dolan had been shot and was dying, so she's on her way back here. Dolan's life is not in danger, and he won't tell me what's going on. He came into town earlier with some gun help, and a couple of men were shot and killed. Dolan reckons he was trying to clean out some of the bad men.'

119

'He's been on this range for about three years,' Hannah mused. 'He runs a tough outfit, but who doesn't these days?'

'There's a glut of bad men in the county, and something out of the ordinary must have attracted them. I'm certain Dolan is mixed up in it somewhere, judging from what little he has said. Have you any idea where he came from and what he did before he arrived?'

'There has been talk but I wouldn't take any serious notice of it because there's no proof, although you don't get smoke without fire. His outfit killed John Twitchett, one of his smaller neighbours. They said they caught him rustling Dolan's stock, and Sheriff Bain said there was evidence to prove Twitchett's guilt.'

'I would discount anything the sheriff said,' Banham mused. 'When I check him out I expect to find he was in cahoots with the men causing the trouble.'

'Dolan has managed to keep his past a secret, and that is suspicious in itself.' She shook her head. 'I can't tell you anything, Dale.'

'Don't worry about it. I'll have to do my job the hard way. Will you be OK now?'

Hannah nodded. Her eyes were over-bright. She sighed. Banham squeezed her arm gently.

'I have to go. I'll see you tomorrow, but I'm gonna be real busy from here on in.'

'So what's new?' she smiled wanly, got up when he arose, and walked with him to the door. 'Take care of yourself, Dale. I should think this is one of the toughest jobs you've ever faced.'

'You can say that again.' He kissed her cheek. 'So long!'

Walking back to the law office, he considered the situation, and tried to think of a way to break the deadlock. On a hunch, he went along the street to the doctor's house. Palmer was in his office, bandaging a young boy's right leg.

'You were lucky this time, Jimmy,' Palmer was saying to the boy. 'In future you'd better not climb trees until you're much older.'

'I wouldn't have climbed that one, Doc, if our cat hadn't shinned up it and got stuck.'

Palmer turned his attention to Banham.

'How's Dillman, Doc?' Banham asked. 'I'd like to ask him some questions, if he's conscious.'

'Let's go see him.' Palmer said. 'I must tell you that his chances of surviving have lessened since he came in. He's feverish, and that ain't good.' He placed a hand on the boy's shoulder. 'Come on, Jimmy. You can sit in my kitchen until your mother comes to collect you.'

Dillman was in a bed in a small back room. He was unconscious, breathing tortuously. Sweat shone on his pallid face. A trickle of blood showed at a corner of his mouth. He was restless. His lips moved but he made no sound.

'He sure as hell look like he's on the down slope,' Banham observed. 'I didn't think his wound was too bad.'

'The bullet nicked his lung.' Palmer wiped the blood from Dillman's mouth. 'I don't think you're gonna be able to talk to him. He probably won't regain consciousness. You'll be wasting your time if you wait around for him to open his eyes.'

'Keep me informed of his condition, Doc,' said Banham as he took his leave to return to the law office.

Entering the jail, he paused on the threshold. The office was silent and still. He went through to the cells and found Dolan lying on his bunk, restless and impatient.

'I want to do a deal, Marshal.' Dolan got off the bunk, groaning in pain as he moved.

'Sure. What have you got to deal with?'

'You turn me loose and I'll get some of the bad men causing the trouble.'

'You're wasting my time.' Banham turned to leave.

'Wait a minute. I'll give you information on what is going on around here.'

'I'm listening.'

'Do we have a deal?'

'Give me some details and I'll judge whether you've got anything to deal with.'

'You're a tough man, Marshal. OK, I'm desperate enough to go along with you. My daughter is a stake in this business. I told you Dillman is a gang boss, and I heard that Snap Miner is planning to bring his boys in to join with him.'

'What's the interest around here? Why would

they risk their liberty on this range? Has someone local got a secret gold mine?'

'I'm still trying to get the lowdown on that. You arrived on the scene, and a lot of men are dead because of you. You shoot too straight, Marshal. You need to take a prisoner or two so you can ask questions and get the answers that matter.'

'You don't have anything to deal with, Dolan.' Banham turned away again. 'I've got better things to do than listen to you.'

'Wait,' Dolan called, desperation suddenly edging his tone.

Banham ignored him and went back into the office. He sat down behind the desk, put his elbows on the paper-strewn surface, and lowered his aching head into his cupped hands. He closed his eyes, and was thinking that he could sleep the clock around when the crash of a shot along the street had him leaping out of the chair and hurrying to the door. He hit the sidewalk at a run, his right hand on the butt of his holstered gun, his headache pushed into the background by the exigencies of the moment.

Gun smoke was drifting along the street near the saloon. A saddled horse was moving across the street opposite the saloon, trailing its reins, and no sign of its rider. Movement caught Banham's gaze and he saw two riders sitting on their mounts motionless at the end of the street where the livery barn was situated. Both had guns in their hands. Banham heaved a sigh and started towards them. The two riders swung their mounts and moved on out of town. He continued to the saloon.

He collected the loose horse and tied it to the hitch rail in front of the saloon, checked the animal for a brand, and saw a Big D on its rump. He gave a sigh of impatience at the sight of it, and wondered if some of Dolan's surviving men were planning to break the rancher out of jail. He entered the saloon, which was practically deserted, and crossed to the bar to talk to the bartender, a tall lean man with a knife scar on his left cheek.

'Did you hear that shot a couple of minutes ago?' Banham demanded.

'Sure I heard it. I'm not deaf,' the tender replied. 'There's been so much shooting around here lately no one bothers to check on it now.'

'Has anyone entered or left the saloon before or after the shot?'

'Not to my knowledge. We're very quiet this time of the day.'

Banham glanced around the big room. Four men were at a small table, intent on their game of poker. A cowboy was standing at the far end of the bar with a half-empty glass of beer before him. Banham turned and went back out to the sidewalk.

A few curious men were in evidence, looking around for the source of the shot. Banham ignored them and went to the alley beside the saloon. He walked to the far end, which gave him a view of the unlovely back lots. They were deserted. He went back to the main street and headed for the law office.

When a voice called to him from the alley beside the jail, Banham turned sharply to look for the source of the voice, and saw the muzzle of a pistol pointing at him.

'Don't do anything with your hands,' the voice commanded. 'Come into the alley.'

Banham held his hands away from his waist. He had no option but to obey and went into the alley, body tensed for a slug in the belly. . . .

NINE

A small man was holding the gun, and he moved back into the alley as Banham advanced into it. Banham looked at the wrinkled face behind the gun and a pang of recognition stabbed through him. The man was well under six feet in height. A flat plains hat covered his greying hair. He seemed jumpy, nervous, although the muzzle of his gun was steady, like a barn door.

'Al Bender. What are you doing in these parts?' Banham demanded. 'And what's with the gun? Are you fixing to shoot me?'

'Not me! Two of Dillman's gang are after me. They took a shot at me as I came into town a few minutes ago. I heard you was back in this neck of the woods, and I need your protection.'

'I saw two riders on the edge of town but they skedaddled when I tried to get close to them. They're gone now. Why are they after you?'

'I overheard something that Dillman wants kept secret so he sent two of his boys to take care of me.

If you'll put me in one of your cells I'll tell you what I heard Dillman talking about. It'll interest you.'

'Has he come to this range in competition with the other outlaws moving in?'

'Yeah. The pickings are rich, and Dillman wants it all for himself. Say, can't we get under cover? I feel kind of naked, out here like this with a couple of killers looking for me. Put me in one of your cells and I'll be able to breathe easier. You ain't forgetting that you owe me a favour, huh?'

'I've got a long memory, Al, and I seem to recollect that somewhere back along the trail you once saved my life. Sure, I owe you one. Are you planning to stay long?'

'Only until you've shot the hell out of the outlaws.'

'I can't do anything yet. I don't know what's going on around here, and my hands are tied until I get the lowdown. Come on into the law office and we'll talk.'

Banham turned to leave the alley but Bender shook his head.

'I'll come in the back door,' he said. 'I don't want the wrong eyes to see where I'm gonna hit the sack.'

'I don't want you out of my sight now that I've seen you,' Banham said. 'Come on, no one will get to you while I'm around.'

Banham produced the office door key as he gained the sidewalk, and when he unlocked the door Bender slipped past him like a wraith and hurried into the office. Banham entered and locked

127

the door. He sat down behind the desk and indicated the chair opposite.

'Take the weight off your feet, Al, and start talking.'

Bender looked around the office, noting the position of the desk and checking the big front window. He moved the chair slightly before sitting down, and then glanced around again, checking his position before relaxing and facing Banham.

'So what's drawing all the bad men to this range, Al?'

'Money! What else.'

'There's no big money in this neck of the woods. There's only the bank, and there's nothing special about that. What's got the bad men ruffling their feathers?'

'It's obvious you haven't heard about it. There's talk that dough to the tune of over one hundred thousand dollars is salted away around here somewhere.'

'You've got to be joking. If there was that kind of money around here then my department would have got wind of it.' Banham leaned forward and propped his elbows on the desk. He gazed intently into Bender's eyes. 'OK, you've got my interest so spill the beans.'

'Big Boy Hayes, who operated a gang in the west of Kansas a few years ago, dropped out of sight with all the dough he stole from God only knows how many trains he robbed over the years. He disappeared without trace, and anyone who is anyone riding the owl hoot trail has kept an eye open for him, all of them with the intention of grabbing his dough for themselves.'

'I heard about Hayes,' Banham mused. 'He ran Jesse James and his bunch a close second with his raids. Are you saying Hayes is hiding out around here, with all his dough?'

'He sure wouldn't leave his wealth lying around after all the risks he took to get it. He killed his original gang because they weren't happy with him taking off with their share of the stolen dough. They say Hayes buried all of them between Dodge City and Nebraska. But Tom Bullen got away. I met him in Nevada and he told me about it. I decided to grab some of that loot for myself, but I got myself in trouble with Dillman's outfit when I arrived, with the result that I've got two killers looking for me to pin my ears back. So here I am, hoping to call in the favour you owe me.'

'So where is Big Boy Hayes now?' Banham asked.

'He's burrowed himself into this community, and doing pretty good for himself.'

'I don't know Hayes personally, and I expect he changed his name when he retired from the owl hoot trail. What is he calling himself now?'

'He bought himself a ranch here about three years ago, changed his name to Dolan, and put one of his gang, Chain Bain, in the town as the sheriff.'

'Dolan! Well what do you know?' Banham exclaimed.

'Have you come across him here?'

'It just so happens I've got him in a cell right now.' Banham picked up the cell keys. 'Come and take a look, and tell me if we're talking about the same man.'

They went into the cells, and Bender peered between the bars of Dolan's cell. Dolan was asleep on his bunk, snoring softly, his mouth agape.

'That's Big Boy Hayes,' Bender said in an undertone. He saw the blood-stained bandage on Dolan's shoulder. 'Did you shoot him?'

'I did. Where has he cached his dough?'

'That's the rub. He's keeping word of that close to his vest. If he's taken by one of the gangs nosing around they'll soon sweat the truth out of him – before they kill him.'

'He's staying right where he is, and no one will get to him. When I get the dough it will go back to its rightful owners, if I have anything to do with it.'

'You'll have to do something about Dolan's daughter if you want to keep control of Dolan.'

'What do you know about Julie Dolan?'

'There's a man on the range who's thrown in his lot with Dolan – Jake Dillman – the foreman out at Big D, and he's making a play for the cache. He's using Julie Dolan as a lever against Dolan. And that ain't all. There's a tough crook hiding out in town, and he's been trying to get on the inside with Dolan. He's been here a lot longer than Dolan. The Dolan girl has been in Austin a couple of years, getting educated. Now Dillman is bringing her back, and if Dolan wants to see her alive again he'll have to part with his money.'

'So that's the way they're playing it. Dolan said he got a wire today from Austin telling him that a man saw Julie and told her Dolan had been shot and was dying. She upped and headed back this way. Do you know her whereabouts?'

'I reckon she'll be held by Dillman.'

'I shot Dillman. He's at the doc's place, and the last I heard he isn't expected to see the sun go down.'

'You've been real busy. So what are you gonna do now?'

'Who is the local man who has thrown in with Dolan?'

'You got a one-track mind, Marshal. Before we do a deal, what's in it for me? You're the law around here, and I know you'll always play it by the book. But I've got a lot of time tied up in this thing now, plus I've got a couple of killers just aching to line up their guns on me, so I'll keep some of my information back in case I need to make a fresh deal.'

'You'll come out of it with your life, Al, and that's the best I can do for you. Ain't your life worth that much?'

'I guess it is, if you put it like that.'

'It's the only deal I can offer you, being who I am. If I come out on top of this trouble then there'll be a reward for the return of the dough Dolan has got stashed away, and I don't see why it shouldn't fall into your lap. That's the deal, plain and simple. So how does it sound to you?'

'OK, so deal me in. You keep the killers off my neck and I get any reward. That ain't bad, Marshal. Here's my hand on it.'

They shook hands, and Banham retained his hold on Bender's limp fingers.

'So give me all the information you have, and it better be value for money. Play it straight, Al, and I'll back you all the way.'

'The big man in town was once in Dolan's gang; they ran the outfit together, but that was way back. He left Dolan and came here to set up a safe place for Dolan when things got too hot for the gang, and it worked out the way they wanted. Dolan finally settled down here, and Abel Stagg paved the way for him, but Stagg didn't bargain for Dolan keeping all the dough he'd saved.'

'Stagg obviously changed his name when he came here,' Banham said impatiently. 'What is he called now? Tell me and I'll slap him behind bars where he belongs.'

Bender grimaced and shook his head. 'I know I can trust you, Marshal, and I'm putting my life in your hands. But I'd feel a lot happier if I hang on to something I can bargain with, if the worst comes to the worst, so if you won't mind if I keep Stagg's real name to myself until the game is over.'

'And if you happen to collect a slug in the meantime then I'll lose out on hauling in the biggest fish in the pond. That doesn't sound good to me.'

'As I see it, the minute I die the whole deal is off anyway.'

Banham nodded. 'OK let's look at the rest of the trouble. Dillman started off around here because he wanted Dolan's hidden dough. No doubt he helped to amass it in the first place. Now Dillman is out of it, and if he survives he'll face twenty years in prison. So name the bad men who are left. I need to deal with them.'

'You've already shot the hell out of them, and now Dillman is on his last trail the rest will pull out pretty damn quick. Any who stay in the hope of getting their hands on Dolan's cache will be out at Big D. All you've got to do is take a posse out there and clean up.'

'Until now, I haven't been able to see the wood for the trees,' Banham mused. 'The way you put it there's not much left for me to do. But I can't believe that. Tell me more about Dolan's cache. Why didn't he put that dough in a bank? It would be safer there than being buried.'

'The kind of money Dolan has isn't so easy to put into a bank account. Any banker would be suspicious, and he'd guess right if he suspected it was stolen.'

'I'll have to lock you in a cell,' Banham decided. 'I can't have you getting under my feet, and I need to keep an eye on you all the time.'

'No need to lock me up,' Bender said sharply. 'You could take me on as a jailer.'

Banham shook his head. 'There's a special cell on the upper floor, so that's where you'll go. I don't want you mixing with Dolan. He's getting mighty impatient now, what with his daughter being brought back here to add to his problems, and if he saw you running around in here he might be tempted to try to make a deal with you. Come on. Let's get you put away. Then I can get on with my duty.'

Bender protested but Banham was adamant, and when he had locked Bender in the upstairs cell he went to see Dolan again. The Big D rancher was on his feet, pacing his cell like a caged tiger. When he heard the noise of the door leading into the cells from the office being opened he lurched to the door of his cell and grasped the bars with his uninjured left hand. Banham entered and confronted him, jingling the bunch of keys.

'It's time you told me the truth,' Banham said without preamble. 'I've been hearing about how you moved into your ranch, and I know about the cache of dough you've got hidden away someplace. You told me about Dillman using your daughter as a lever against you, and if the telegram you got from Austin informing you that your girl is on her way back here now is correct then time is running out and you'll be pressed into revealing where your cache is. Bear in mind that your daughter's life is at stake. You know your gang better than anyone, so I don't have to paint you a picture of what will happen to her if you don't come up with your loot. Your only chance now is to throw in your lot with me.'

'You're a lawman! I'll lose everything if I trust you.'

134

'Look at it this way, Dolan. You lost everything from the moment I locked you in here. What you have to concentrate on now is picking up the pieces of what you had, and your daughter's life should be at the top of the list. If I were in your boots I wouldn't have to think twice about what to do. So why are you stalling? Get it into your head that you've lost the game and you've got to make the best deal you can. Make no mistake about it. I'll come out on top in the end so you'll have nothing left, and you might even lose your life in my clean-up.'

'Let me think some more about it.' Dolan turned away from the door to drop on to his bunk.

Banham looked at him for several minutes, then sighed and went back in the front office. He heard someone knocking at the street door, and loosened his pistol in its holster as he went to answer. He jerked open the door and was surprised to see Aggie, Hannah's friend, standing unsteadily on the boardwalk, leaning heavily on a long gun.

'Aggie, what are you doing here?' He stepped outside and grasped her arm, for she looked in danger of falling. Her face was pale and her blue eyes showed she was feverish, and he could not forget that she had been shot trying to cover his back. He led her into the office and sat her down on a seat. 'Are you loco, disobeying Doc's orders? He told you to rest.'

'Hannah has gone back to the ranch, Dale. I tried to stop her but she's in shock over Larry's death. You'll have to go after her. It isn't safe for her to be out alone. Fetch her back, and be quick, before those gunnies latch on to her.'

'I should have guessed she'd do something like this.' Banham suppressed a sigh. 'Come on, I'll see you back to the store and then I'll go after her.'

'I can make it home alone,' she said firmly. 'Please hurry after Hannah.'

He helped her out of the office and watched her totter along the sidewalk back towards the general store before he locked the office and went in the opposite direction to the hotel. He could not leave the law office unattended, and Frank Parfitt, the town mayor, seemed to be the only man in town in a position to help him.

Parfitt was in his office when Banham went into the hotel.

'I've got to leave town, and it's urgent,' Banham said. 'I can't leave the office unattended. Can you help?'

'I'll take over until you get back,' Parfitt said. 'What you should do is send to your head office for some gun help.'

'I've almost got this trouble sorted out. I believe I can handle it. But I can't be in two places at once.' He handed Parfitt the office keys and departed, eager to get after Hannah. . . .

Impatience gnawed at him until he was out on the trail to the ranch. He rode at a gallop, his mind filled with images of Hannah alone and at the mercy of those human wolves preying on this range.

An hour later he spotted Hannah's rig ahead.

The horses were trotting, lifting their knees high, and Hannah was not observing her surroundings. She sat slumped on the driving seat, shoulders hunched and head forward. Banham touched spurs to his horse and began to overhaul the rig. He was instinctively vigilant from long experience, and when three riders swept over a ridge ahead and galloped to surround the rig he reached for his gun.

He was spotted before he could draw within range, and the three gunmen reacted swiftly. One grasped the reins of Hannah's horse and set off back the way he had come, taking the rig and Hannah with him. The other two riders turned to confront Banham. Gun smoke flared when they started shooting, and hot lead flew around him as the noise of the gunshots rolled across the range.

Banham settled himself in his saddle, trying to minimise his target area. He held his pistol in his right hand, but was more intent on getting to closer quarters, until a bullet slashed across his neck, leaving a burn on his flesh. He triggered his Colt and one of the riders slid out of his saddle.

The rig disappeared over the ridge. Banham threw down on the second rider and squeezed his trigger. The rider changed direction immediately, pulling on his reins and slewing his horse to his left. Banham fired another shot, and saw the rider quit his saddle and cartwheel along the ground before coming to rest inertly in the long grass.

Banham urged his horse to greater effort. He galloped over the ridge, saw the rig containing

Hannah being urged along at a much faster pace, and set off in pursuit. Gun echoes were fading into the vast distance. Banham was perturbed when he couldn't see Hannah sitting on her seat, and he used his spurs mercilessly as he gave chase.

The effort of chasing Hannah increased the headache Banham was suffering, which had started when he was struck on the head as he was taken prisoner by Hogan's men. When his horse stumbled and fell, he kicked his feet out of the stirrups and vacated the saddle, pitching helplessly to the ground. He landed heavily and a flash seemed to ignite threads of agony in his head. Blackness darker than the night surged up from within him. Sight and consciousness left him and he lay as if dead while the rig took his sister from the scene. . . .

Banham came back to his senses. He sat up before opening his eyes, and when he peered at his surroundings he discovered that the range was undulating in great waves. He closed his eyes and then reopened them, and his wavering gaze alighted on a figure standing near him. He grabbed for his pistol instinctively to find his holster was empty, and he sagged when he recognized Aggie's voice.

'What are you doing here?' he demanded.

'It's a good thing I decided to trail you,' she replied. 'There are two dead men close by, so you've been busy, but where is Hannah?'

'A third man was taking her away while I dealt with those other two, and when I gave chase my horse fell.' While he was explaining, Banham kept his eyes closed, but opened them again them immediately. 'Bring your horse beside me,' he told her. 'I need to get on my feet.'

She fetched her horse, and when Banham reached out an unsteady hand she grasped his wrist and guided his fingers to the stirrup. He dragged himself upright and leaned against the horse while he tried to gather his balance. It took him several minutes before his senses settled and he could open his eyes fully and look around normally.

'What are you going to do now?' Aggie demanded.

'I've got to go after Hannah.'

'You'd better take my horse.' She looked around, located his pistol and picked it up. He took it and thrust it into his holster. 'We're not far from your ranch now, so I'll walk in there and get another horse.'

'And then go back to town out of this,' he said sharply. 'I've got enough trouble on my plate without having you to worry about.'

'The boot is on the other foot,' she replied. 'I'm worried about you.'

He paused and looked at her. He could see she was worried, and he moistened his lips and sighed.

'I'm sorry,' he said. 'Don't think I'm not grateful, but I'm up to my neck at the moment.'

'So why are you standing here?' she countered.

'You can come with me. We'll ride double to the ranch.'

He swung into her saddle and took his left foot out of the stirrup. Aggie grasped his knee and slid her toe into the vacant stirrup. A gasp of pain escaped her as the movement put pressure on her wound. It was with great difficulty that she got behind the saddle. She clung to him as he kicked the horse into movement.

Banham found it difficult to go on. A buzzing sound in his ears warned him of impending trouble. His head was throbbing insistently, and any slight movement he made had a bad effect on his sense of balance. When he began to lean sideways without being aware of the movement Aggie tightened her grip around his waist and spoke sharply in his ear.

'You're not fit enough to do this, Dale.'

'I'll manage,' he replied. 'There's no one else to do it.'

They were silent until they reached the ranch, and Banham reined up at the gate to the yard. He made an effort to look around, and disappointment filled him when he saw the place was deserted. There was no sign of life, and Hannah's rig was not evident. Aggie slid off the back of the horse and opened the gate.

'Ride to the porch and stay there while I take a look around,' she said, and Banham did not object. She walked beside him when he crossed the yard, and when he reined in at the house she went ahead to look around, a pistol in her hand.

Banham remained in the saddle, his eyes closed. Time passed unnoticed, and he jerked into full alertness when Aggie spoke to him from the doorway to the house.

'There's been no one here since we left,' she called. 'We'll have to check the trail for tracks. As I see it, a gunman wouldn't bring Hannah here. He's probably one of Dolan's bunch, and he'll have gone back to Big D.'

'Stay here and I'll take a look.' Banham gathered up the reins and rode back across the yard. He stiffened in the saddle and brought his mind to bear on what he had to do. He rode to the main trail, which went by the ranch a few hundred yards out, and he was relieved when he looked around and discovered that his head was improving. His sight had almost returned to normal and there was just a dull ache inside his head.

He found the rig's wheel tracks on the trail, heading in the direction of Dolan's spread. He returned to the ranch, where Aggie was standing on the porch.

'It looks like Hannah is being taken to Dolan's ranch,' he told her. 'Collect a horse and we'll get going.'

'Not so fast. I've made some coffee. Come and have a cup. You look like Old Nick himself.'

'I'm feeling better,' he protested, but slid out of the saddle and trailed the reins. He almost lost his balance as he mounted the porch steps, and Aggie ran to him and grasped his arm to steady him.

They went into the house and he sat down at the kitchen table. Aggie poured coffee and joined him.

141

She drank quickly, draining her cup, and then got up.

'I'll saddle a horse for you,' she said. 'We need to get on Hannah's tracks.'

'You're not going with me.' His tone brooked no argument. 'I'll push on and do what I have to do.'

'If you think I'll let you go alone in your condition then you're not the man Hannah says you are. Don't be pig-headed, Dale. I'm gonna tag along, and there's nothing more to be said.'

He poured another cup of coffee while Aggie was getting a horse for him, and she brought a mount round to the porch. Banham could hear her voice when she spoke, and a man answered. Banham got to his feet in a rush, drew his gun, and was covering the door when Aggie crossed the porch and came in, followed closely by a big brute of a man. They both halted and stared at Banham's levelled pistol.

'Ease up, Dale,' said Aggie, stepping in front of the stranger. 'This is Al Carson from town. Hannah saw him the other evening and arranged for him to come in here daily and do the chores, feeding the stock and such like.'

Banham holstered his pistol and went forward with outstretched hand. Carson shook hands, smiling, and Banham saw respect in his blue eyes.

'Hannah told me all about you, Marshal,' Carson said. 'I'm doing a good job here. Hannah told me to expect trouble, but I haven't seen a soul, which doesn't surprise me from what I've heard about the trouble in town. You've been shooting bad men like

142

there's no tomorrow. I heard before I left town that Dillman, Dolan's ramrod, died at the doc's place. Never took him to be an outlaw. And just as I turned off the main trail coming here I saw Dolan riding out to his place. He was heavily bandaged, but he was hammering along like a cowhand heading for a round-up.'

'I left Dolan in jail when I rode out,' Banham said sharply, 'and the town mayor was gonna stand by in the law office to take care of things. I sure wish I could be in two places at once. But I'm going out to Dolan's spread now, and I'd better split the breeze, but fast.'

He ran out to the porch, his physical problems pushed into the back of his mind, and sprang into the saddle of the horse Aggie had got him. He went across the yard like a blue streak, and glanced over his shoulder as he hit the trail to Dolan's place to see Aggie following him at a gallop. He stifled a groan because, knowing what he had to do, Aggie's presence could only add to his problems. . . .

TEN

By the time Banham set eyes on Big D the reaction of his efforts had caught up with him and he felt weak and unsteady. But he did not pause, and rode toward the ranch, selecting a path that gave him a covered approach. He circled the ranch house. Hannah's rig was standing beside the barn. He dismounted and left his horse inside the barn. There was movement just outside when he eased out of the barn, and he swung quickly to face it, his pistol coming to hand, his index finger trembling on the trigger. He heaved a sigh. It was Aggie, leading her horse, and he stood motionless while she put the animal under cover.

When she joined him, a rifle in her hands, he opened his mouth to chide her but closed it again, aware that she would ignore him. She gazed at him with defiance in her eyes but she was trembling, and looked as if she would collapse at any moment.

'I reckon there are better things you could be doing, like resting in bed,' he said.

'There'll be time enough for that later,' she countered. 'Hannah is here so what are you waiting for?'

'Don't push me,' he retorted. 'You're holding me up, distracting me when I need a clear mind. Wait here and I'll see if I can get Hannah out of the house. Then you and she can head back to town pronto, and stay in the store until I show up. I'm going into the house, and you stay here no matter what happens. I don't want you getting caught up in any action. Try to act like a normal woman for once and give me a break.'

Aggie opened her mouth to speak, but she turned away, a hurt expression on her face, and went back into the barn. Banham hoped she would stay there, and moved on, his expression tightening as he walked determinedly to the back door of the house, his pistol steady in his hand.

The back door was barred. He tried several times to open it before giving up, and he knew he would have to do this the hard way. He went to the rear corner of the house and peered out from its cover at the rear of the spread. There were two corrals out that way, also a bunk house and the cook's shack. A man was beside one of the corrals, which contained ten horses, and Banham kept a close eye on him while he walked along the side of the ranch house to its front corner.

When he reached the side of the porch he paused to peer around, checking the yard and the front of the house. Two saddle horses were tied to a rail in front of the porch, and one of them looked as if it had been hard ridden. He approached one of the two front windows and edged forward to look into the house. Two men were inside the big front room, and one of them was Dolan, slumped on a big leather settee, looking as if the hard ride from town had exhausted him. There was a sheen of sweat on his face and he looked pale and drawn. The other man was big, tough-looking, and Banham saw that he was wearing two pistols around his waist on crossed gun-belts, and guessed he was the man who had brought Hannah here.

It was in Banham to enter the house immediately and re-arrest Dolan, but at the moment he could think only of Hannah. Once she was safe he could do his duty. He backed off the porch and checked the side of the house. A lean-to shed towards the rear corner had an upper window just above it, and there were several bales of straw stacked against the wall of the shed. He steeled himself to make an effort and mounted the bales to haul his protesting body on to the roof of the lean-to. The building protested at his weight, and he crawled to the window.

The window was ajar and he swung it open and slid over the sill into a bare room. He tiptoed to the door and moved out into a narrow passage and eased toward the front rooms. Silence lay heavily over the house, and heat was packing the interior. He went to the nearest door, found it was locked, and saw a key hanging on a nail beside the door. When he opened the door he saw Hannah in the room, seated on a bed. She was hunched over with her hands to her face.

'Hannah, come on, let's get out of here,' he said softly.

She looked up, and gazed at him for some moments as if unable to believe her eyes. Then she got to her feet and hurried to him, throwing her arms around his neck.

'Dale, I knew you'd come looking for me.'

'We've got to get out of here. Aggie is down in the barn, and she's going to take you back to town. I've got things to do here and I need to get started pronto.'

He led her to the door and paused to look down into her shimmering eyes.

'Quiet now, and do exactly what I tell you,' he urged.

She nodded, and he went on, with Hannah following him closely. They went to the stairs and descended to the lower floor. The stairs creaked despite his efforts to remain silent, and when he paused on the ground floor he could hear voices coming from the big front living room. Hannah joined him, and he indicated that she should precede him to the kitchen. He followed her, watching his back, his pistol ready for action. In a few moments they were clear of the house and he led her to the barn, where Aggie was waiting impatiently. The two women embraced, but Banham interrupted them, urging them to hurry.

'Take my horse, Hannah,' he said. 'Head back to

town, and stay off the main trail. When you get to the store just stay there until I get back. Promise me you'll obey me.'

They both agreed, and Banham was impatient until they were mounted and on their way. He stood watching their departure until they were clear, and then his manner changed and he stiffened to do his job. He checked his pistol as he returned to the ranch house, but a man opened the kitchen door as Banham passed, and stepped outside. He was holding a rifle, wore twin pistols around his waist, and Banham recognized him as the man who had been with Dolan in the house.

He turned to face the threat and the man struck at Banham's pistol with the barrel of his rifle. Banham lost his grip on the gun and the man kicked it out of reach.

Banham stepped in close, grasped the barrel of the rifle, jerked it out of the man's hands and received a retaliatory punch that crashed against his jaw. Banham's knees buckled. He threw his arms around the man and hung on as his senses swam. The man brought up his knee to Banham's groin, sending pain flashing through his lower body. Banham butted him in the face, felt the nose crumple as the man jerked away, and Banham stayed close, his feet moving quickly, He threw a series of left and right punches in a powerful tattoo that hammered the man to the ground.

The man started to his feet, but Banham kicked out shrewdly, the toe of his dusty boot connecting with the man's head, and he fell back and slumped on the ground.

Banham picked up his gun and covered the man, who was dressed in range clothes, and waited until he came back to his senses.

'Get up,' Banham ordered, and pushed him in the direction of the barn. He found some rope and hog-tied his prisoner, leaving him with a terse warning. 'Don't make a sound or I'll come back and shoot you.' He paused, and then asked. 'What's your name?'

'Jack Milligan. I work for Dolan.'

'Good enough! Stay quiet until I come back for you.'

Banham circled the house once more, intending to confront Dolan and get the drop on him, but when he reached the side of the porch he drew back into cover. Four riders were coming across the yard, and Banham was horrified when he recognized two of them – Hannah and Aggie. Behind them were two more riders, and Banham was further dismayed when he recognized one as Henry Parfitt. The rider with Parfitt was a young woman, and she and Parfitt were chatting animatedly as they reined up and dismounted.

Banham stared at Parfitt, shocked to see him, wondering who was taking care of the law office back in town. He was tempted to reveal himself instantly, but the two men riding herd on Hannah and Aggie were holding pistols in their hands, and he waited until the group entered the house before moving to the nearest window on the porch to peer into the big room. Dolan was still seated on the couch, and he was staring at the girl with shock on his face. He struggled to get to his feet but the girl ran to him and sat by his side to embrace him. Julie Dolan, Banham thought, home from Austin at last, and he felt sympathy for her because he knew she had a load of grief to face before this business would be concluded.

Hannah and Aggie were cowed by the drawn guns held by their two captors and remained motionless, although Aggie's face was showing her feelings. She was seething with anger.

Banham heard the sound of hoofs approaching across the yard and looked toward the gate to see a rider arriving. He stepped off the porch and again concealed himself behind the corner of the house. The newcomer was dressed in town clothes, and was heavily armed. He dismounted and went into the house. Banham moved back to the window to observe, and saw Parfitt greet the townsman. There had a lively conversation for several moments, and then Parfitt came to the door and opened it. The townsman emerged on to the porch, followed by the four men who had brought Hannah and Aggie back to the ranch. Parfitt stood in the doorway. He seemed to have taken over.

'You men go over to the cook shack and get some grub,' Parfitt said. 'Don't relax because I suspect Marshal Banham is somewhere around, and we want him dead. If he shows up then shoot on sight.

150

He's too dangerous to handle. You got that?'

The men muttered agreement and stepped off the porch to cross the yard to the cook shack. Parfitt went back to Dolan, and Banham returned to the window. There was a conversation between Parfitt and Dolan. Then Parfitt produced a pistol and ushered Hannah and Aggie out of the room, both protesting as they went. Dolan was ill at ease, evidently bothered by his shoulder wound, and his daughter sat attentively by his side.

Banham checked on the movements of the five men going to the cook shack. They were on the point of entering the small building over by the bunk house and, when they disappeared inside, Banham tightened his grip on his pistol, went to the door of the house, and entered.

Dolan sat upright in shock at Banham's appearance, but the sudden movement was too much for him and he fell back and closed his eyes. Julie Dolan sprang to her feet, her gaze on Banham's law badge.

'Are you the man they want to kill?' she demanded.

'They've been trying to kill me ever since I arrived in this neck of the woods,' he responded. 'Are you aware that your father is a wanted outlaw?'

'I've heard rumours, but I haven't had much to do with him over the years. I lived with my mother until she died, and then came here to live when Pa bought this place. Within a year I was sent to Austin to finish my schooling.'

151

'I'm planning to take your father back to jail. Do you have any people around here you could stay with?'

'I'll go back to town and stay there,' she decided. 'Are you going to arrest Mr Parfitt?'

'I expect so. I've got to check him out, but I'm pretty sure he is involved in your father's criminal activities.'

Parfitt returned to the big room, putting his pistol back in his pocket as he did so. He saw Banham and instinctively reached for his gun.

'Don't do it,' Banham said. 'Get your hands up and I'll take your gun.'

Parfitt lifted his hands and Banham relieved him of his pistol.

'Where did you come from?' Parfitt demanded. 'I'm here because I saw Dolan's daughter in town. She got off the stage coach, and looked lost and disturbed, so I offered to escort her out here to her father.'

'That was public-spirited of you,' Banham replied. 'Now tell me how Dolan got out of jail? I left you in charge of the local law when I gave you the jail keys.'

Parfitt remained silent, and Banham laughed.

'I'll get back to you in a moment. First, we'll find out a few facts. Who is the man you sent over to the cook shack? He rode up and came into the house as if he had a right to be here, and you gave him orders to kill me on sight if I showed up.'

'I got nothing to say.' Parfitt spoke stiffly through

lips that seemed frozen in shock.

'OK. I expect you'll change your mind about that by the time I get through with you. So you turned Dolan loose; a man I arrested according to the law. What have you got to say about that?'

Parfitt shook his head. He seemed incapable of speech now. He was sweating, and a hunted expression had appeared in his eyes. He pulled a handkerchief from a pocket and mopped his face – caught red-handed, and his guilt showing plainly.

'I'm looking for a man in town who was in Dolan's gang some time ago – his name was Stagg in those days – before Dolan retired from lawlessness and came to this county to raise cattle. It's beginning to look like you're Stagg, Parfitt, so consider yourself under arrest until I can get around to checking you out. Now let's talk about the money that was stolen from the railroad. There are rumours that you've hidden it around here, Dolan.'

'That's all it is – rumour,' Dolan said.

'That's OK, I'll continue the questioning when we get back to the jail. I'm gonna have to hog-tie you while I get some horses, after I've dealt with the five men over in the cook shack. Where did you put my sister and her friend, Parfitt?'

'They're in a bedroom.' Parfitt was sweating now, and he looked greatly troubled.

Banham saw a lariat hanging on the wall over the fireplace and took it down. He motioned for Parfitt to lie on the floor, and hog-tied him. When he approached Dolan, the rancher protested at being tied, and Banham turned to Julie Dolan.

'Go upstairs and turn my sister and her friend loose, will you?'

She went without protest, and returned shortly with Hannah and Aggie accompanying her. Banham handed Aggie a pistol and she looked at him questioningly.

'Do you want me to shoot somebody?' she asked.

'Do so if you have to. I want you to keep an eye on Dolan while I go for those men out at the cook shack. When I've disarmed them we'll head back to town. I don't want anyone running free out here when we leave.'

Aggie examined the gun and then sat at the table and covered Dolan. 'You can forget about him now. If he so much as bats an eyelid now I'll shoot him.'

Banham checked his gun and carried it in his hand when he moved to the door leading into the kitchen. He paused beside Hannah and touched her on the shoulder.

'Stay close to Aggie,' he said. 'I won't be long.'

Hannah smiled wanly but did not speak. Banham drew a deep breath. He looked at Julie Dolan, who had returned to the father's side, and she seemed submissive. He did not think she would cause trouble. He smiled at Aggie but her concentration was on Dolan, and he departed, grimly determined to do what was necessary to bring this trouble to an end.

He left the house by way of the kitchen door and stood in cover surveying the bunk house and the cook shack. Smoke was billowing out of the stovepipe sticking out of the roof of the shack. He eased away to the right and moved steadily across the back yard, gun steady in his hand, eyes missing nothing as he closed in. He was conscious of the necessity of handling this right, but he had to arrest these men before he could succeed in his investigation.

The cook shack had no windows in its back wall, and he made his approach from that direction, intent on getting the upper hand, watching his surroundings until he was standing against the rear wall of the shack. There were several gaps in the sun-warped boards and he applied an eye to one and peered into the shack. A cook was busy at the stove, and the five men waiting for a meal were sitting around a table.

Banham looked over at the nearby bunk house, and froze when he thought he saw movement through the nearest window. Sunlight was slanting against the glass, making vision almost impossible, but he caught the faint change of shadow as someone peered out and then moved back. He turned instantly and crossed to the bunk house, intent on maintaining surprise.

He threw open the door of the bunk house and lunged inside, gun lifting. A cowboy was standing inside, gun in hand, and he fired a shot the instant Banham walked in on him. Banham threw himself down and a slug bored through the crown of his Stetson. He fired in reply, and as gun thunder disturbed the peace of the afternoon the cowboy's gun spilled out of his hand, then thumped on the wooden floor as he crumpled lifelessly.

Banham sprang up and ran out into the open, his ears ringing from the quick gun blasts. He hurled himself across the intervening space to the cook shack, intent on confronting the gunmen and, when he threw open the door of the shack, several guns blasted, and slugs came splintering through the door, but he was already diving to the ground and the hot lead passed harmlessly above him.

He scrambled up and ran around the front corner of the shack, peered into the building through a side window, and smashed the pane of glass with his gun barrel. He saw the men he wanted to arrest facing the door of the shack, and when the glass shattered they whirled to face it, bringing their guns into play.

Banham worked his gun, and smoke blew back into his face. Two of the men ran to the door and vacated the building. Banham kept shooting until his hammer struck an empty cartridge. He ducked and grabbed some shells from his belt, moving position as he fed them into his smoking weapon. The three men inside the shack were down and finished.

The two men that escaped from the shack came at a run around the front corner, caught a glimpse of Banham diving for the rear corner, and cut loose at him. He twisted towards them and dived headlong into the dirt, gun recoiling in his hand as he worked the trigger, his eyes screwed up against flaring gun smoke.

One of the men went down in a whirl of arms and legs. Banham shifted his aim and fired again. The second man fell away as if he had suddenly lost interest in fighting. Blood flew from his face at it smacked against the sun-baked ground.

Banham peered around, gun ready, but the gun echoes were fading. He pushed cautiously to his feet, teeth clenched resolutely, and at that moment he heard two shots sounding from the direction of the ranch house. He ran toward the house, filled with concern. His feet thudded on the porch and he slammed into the front door with his left shoulder. The door gave way and he shifted his feet quickly to maintain his balance as he entered. The muzzle of his gun swung to cover the figures in the room like a bloodhound searching for scent.

Hannah was sitting at the table, a pistol in her hand covering Henry Parfitt, who was on the floor, still hog-tied, and Dolan was huddled on the couch. Banham halted, pushing back his shoulders, and relief began to seep through him. His experience informed him that apart from going into the details of this crooked business, he had it by the tail with a downward pull.

'So where's Julie and Aggie?' he asked. Neither girl was present in the room. 'And what were those two shots I heard?'

'Julie went out through the kitchen,' Hannah replied. 'Aggie fired two shots over her head when she wouldn't stop.'

'Where's Aggie now?'

'She followed Julie.'

'Heck, I don't want her wandering around outside.' Banham ran into the kitchen. 'There might be some more hard cases around, looking for that cache. Stay where you are, Hannah, and keep those two covered, even though they are tied.'

He hurried out the back door and ran across to the barn. He could hear Aggie and Julie talking as he went into the barn. Aggie was standing just inside, a gun in her hand, and Julie was over in a corner, clearing away an assortment of items – old tools, decrepit saddles, some furniture from the house, and an old wardrobe standing back against the wall.

'What's going on?' Banham demanded.

'Julie reckons she knows where that cache is,' Aggie said.

Julie turned when Banham approached her. 'I've seen my father prowling around in here many times,' she said. 'If he's hidden anything then this is the spot it's likely to be.'

'And you're prepared to hand it over to the law, huh?'

'I am law abiding,' she replied, and added pointedly, 'It is my father who is the outlaw.'

Banham set to eagerly, and soon cleared the area around the wardrobe. A pang of disappointment stabbed through him when he finally looked inside and found it was empty.

'Move it, please,' Julie said.

Banham pushed the wardrobe on its front, lifted the top end, and dragged it away from the wall, revealing several short planks on the ground. When he pulled the planks aside he uncovered a shallow pit containing five pairs of saddle-bags. A grin appeared on his face when he checked the bags and saw that they were filled with paper folding money and gold coins.

'So the rumours were true,' he observed. 'We'd better make tracks now, before anyone else turns up. I saw a buckboard by the cook shack. I'll harness a couple of horses to it and we'll take this cache and the prisoners to town.'

The girls went back to the house while Banham readied the buckboard. He harnessed two horses, hitched them to the buckboard, and drove it to the barn to collect the saddle-bags before moving around to the front of the house. He entered the building, half-expecting to find more trouble, but Parfitt was still hog-tied and Dolan was stretched out on the couch. Aggie and Hannah were seated at the table, both holding pistols.

Banham was throbbing with relief as he manhandled Parfitt and the reluctant Dolan into the buckboard. They began to curse when they saw the saddle-bags. Banham laughed and called Hannah and Aggie out of the house.

'We'll ride in our rig,' Hannah said.

'I'd rather the two of you rode shot-gun on my prisoners while I drive the buckboard,' Banham replied. 'You can collect your rig any time.'

He handed Hannah up to the back of the buckboard and turned to help Aggie aboard, but she

159

pushed him off balance and, as he fell, she fired her pistol at someone behind him. The raucous sound of the gun blotted out what she began to say. He spun around on the ground, reaching for his gun, and saw Milligan, the two-gun man he had left hog-tied in the barn, hunching over with Aggie's slug in his belly.

'He was about to shoot you in the back,' Aggie said. 'Now don't you think it's a good job I'm around?'

Banham got to his feet, shaking his head. He thought he could see what would happen in future. Aggie would always be around. But, strangely, he liked the thought of that, and began to think of how he could work towards a different way of life. Aggie had been growing on him ever since they met, and he knew he could do much worse.

He was exhausted, but did not relax his alertness as they returned to town. He had the rights of the crookedness now, and it would all come out in the wash. He was already looking forward to the future. . . .